Angel's Redemption.

Book Two of the Redemption of the Fallen.

By

Scarlett J Rose.

Cover Design by SJR Covers, using images purchased through depositphotos.com.

Edited by: Susan Horsnell

ISBN-10:0-6480098-1-5

ISBN-13:978-0-6480098-1-8

Published by FAR HORIZONS PUBLISHING.

Info.far.horizons@gmail.com

Dedications

To Susan Horsnell, My Editor, My eternal thanks to you, for your time, dedication and encouragement.

Chiara Beltrami Gottmer, who has been my primary Beta Reader, and who loves my Angels and Demons as much as I do, thank you so much for your epic support.

To my Author Friends, some of whom I have met, others I would give my left nut to meet (Okay, so I don't have them, I'm a chick, but IF I had them, then I"d give the left… or would it be the right one…? Anyways, to my Author Friends, you are amazing, keep doing what you do best, creating words for us all to get lost in, book boyfriends to love, loathe and just want to throw stuff at.

I got mad, mad love for you all.

Peace, Love and Romancey/kickass-type stuff.

Scarlett J Rose.

December 2016

1.

The woman sat before him, perched on the desk in the small office. Her legs crossed provocatively, and her naked body hidden behind a large book. She smiled seductively as he entered.

He narrowed his eyes., One look at her and his lust charged into overdrive. He closed the door, the sound of the lock overloud in the thick silence of the room.

"Amy..." His voice and the growing bulge in his pants revealed his want.

"Thomas," Amy's voice purred with sexual hunger.

She tossed aside the book, revealing the soft curves of her breasts, nipples budded in the chill of the office. Uncrossing her legs revealed a pussy bare of hair. Her eyes were locked on him, the object of her desire. She watched him closely and smiled when he responded to her state of undress and sexual readiness for him.

His breathing quickened as she slipped from the desk and padded closer to him. Her deft hands quickly unbuttoned his shirt. She pressed her soft red lips against his hard pectoral muscles, her tongue teased his nipple into an erect bud to match her own.

"Are you...?" he began, but she hushed him, a finely manicured finger pressed softly to his lips.

"I want this, you want me..." She pressed her body to his and her hands dipped down to unfasten his pants. "Why deny the desire between us?"

He groaned as she freed his hard cock, took it into her hands and stroked the head with a fingertip, smearing the dewy bead of pre-cum over the head. Thomas bit his lip and shuddered in torturous pleasure.

"Jenna told me about the little private 'Bible study' session the two of you enjoyed the other day." Amy knelt before him and licked a fresh bead of moisture from the slit at the head.

He groaned and his legs trembled as she caressed him.

"I was hoping we could come to a similar... arrangement." She opened her mouth and took him deep, her tongue licked along his length. His moans of pleasure spurring her on.

Thomas could take no more. With a hoarse roar he exploded, his seed spurted down the back of Amy's throat. He gripped her blonde hair and pulled her from his cock. She licked her lips, the mere sight turning him hard again. He reached down and lifted the naked woman into his arms, carried her to the desk and lowered her, stomach down. Positioning himself behind her, he used his knees to spread her legs. She moaned as he entered her.

Warm, wet and welcoming, her pussy greeted his shaft as he thrust into her. Soft moans gave way to ecstatic cries of pleasure as she pushed back into each thrust. Her generous breasts pooled on the polished wood of the desk as he pounded her, harder and faster as his own climax rushed in on him.

His wings opened above them in all their spectacular glory. They fluttered and trembled as he came with a roar. She followed him over with a climaxing scream.

Behind him. Unseen. A white feather turned jet black and floated to the ground. Fell free from his glorious outstretched wings.

Another Angel on his way to join the ranks of the fallen.

Thomas bolted upright, his eyes blinked rapidly as he adjustied to the darkness. His cock stood at attention thanks to his dream. Though in truth, it was more a memory. He wondered what had woken him, when he heard the distinctive, high-pitched scream of a woman in distress. He sprang to his feet and adjusted himself before bolting from the safety of the old overpass and heading toward the frantic screams.

Dried grass and dirt crunched beneath his feet as he rushed to an abandoned house. The woman's screams echoed through the still of the night. Voices of men joined the noise. He crept quietly to the house where a single candle burned in one of the rooms. Peering through the window, he saw shadows dance on the wall.. His blood boiled with anger as he witnessed the scene before him.

A young woman was held down on the filthy floor by three men. Stripped of her clothing, she struggled futilely against them.

"Let me go!" she screamed, her voice hoarse.

"Nah, I think we'll keep you, have some fun. Right boys?" One of the men spoke as the others lifted her onto the table and flipped her onto her stomach.

"Oh yes." The man removed his pants, exposing his pale, white buttocks to the candlelight. "We're going to have some fun with you." His hand reached out and he caressed the woman's ass.

She whimpered and kicked out in an attempt to connect with his crotch. The man grabbed her foot and held it tightly. "I see you're really into this." His tone was sadistic.

Thomas could not allow these men to violate the woman. He drew his sword and stepped back into the darkness to wait for the perfect moment to strike.

Grace's heart hammered against her chest. Adrenaline and fear coursed through her veins as she struggled against her captors. Her mission to find her sister, Ebony, could not end this way.

The sisters had escaped an attack on their small town of survivors. The gates had been breached by a group of raiders in the middle of the night. Grace and Ebony had fled through a hidden back gate with a group of other survivors, mostly women and children. Running until they were exhausted, theyslept in an old rest stop.

They had awoken surrounded by slavers, with a Demon as their leader. The Slavers had taken Ebony along with several other girls when they had ambushed them.

It still shocked her that, not even a year had passed since the destructive chaos and men had descended into the madness of the world today. There were a few precious cities where the surviving armies of Heaven and Hell had integrated themselves with human society. But, there were far more which hadn't and had disintegrated into the ways of violent anarchy. It was every man, woman and child for themselves.

Humans had returned to their baser natures in the blink of an eye. While most of the survivors had slept, Grace had headed to a roadhouse a few miles away to scavenge for supplies. She hadn't heard the screams until it was too late to help. She'd hidden and watched helplessly as the slavers rounded up each member of the group, Ebony included, and put them all in chains and lengths of rope under heavy armed guard.

Grace had crept along behind them at a safe distance, trying to figure out a way to rescue her sister and the others. To her dismay, she realised they were heading back to their old city, back to the Demons.

She had double backed to the abandoned farmhouse, hoping to find some kind of weapon she could use against the slavers. Each captor had a gun, a baseball or cricket bat or something which could be used as a weapon. She had nothing but a few salvaged tin cans of questionable food and a few bottles of water which had been missed in the initial looting and panic after the war of Heaven and Hell.

Some labelled the war Armageddon, but the world hadn't ended. Most called it the War of the Titans. It was a battle in which no-one had triumphed. At the height of the battle, the Light of Goodness and the Spirit of Darkness had come together and fought in the skies high above. With a thunderous peal, they had vanished, leaving many of their warriors, both Angels and Demons, dead or insane.

Demons who had survived insanity had banded together, determined to dominate the world and every living soul in it. Angels became patrons of churches and lived happily amongst humans, sometimes leading resistance against the Demons. Unfortunately, it appeared, less Angels had survived the destruction and were outnumbered by Demons.

Grace had never killed a man before, never met one who deserved to die. Until now. Now, she had met ten. Three who had ambushed her, held her down and attempted to violate her. And, seven who had snatched her sister and the others and were delivering them to their new lives as slaves. A Demon could be counted amongst her foes and they were much harder to kill than a man.

Grace fought desperately against the firm grip of the bastards who held her face down on the wooden table. The air of the old house was musty and cold on her naked flesh. Her body stuck to the cheap varnish of the tabletop as she sweated with fear. Dust motes flew through the air as she gasped for breath. Her heart hammered against her ribs.

"Let me go!" Her screams were met with cruel laughter and evil taunts. She fought hard, kicked out in an attempt to connect with the balls of the man holding her from behind. Her foot was captured and held out painfully behind her.

His hands danced up her leg and over her ass. She shuddered in revulsion. "Fuck you, you sick fucks. If I ever get free I'll castrate the lot of you." Spittle flew from her lips as she struggled.

Laughter erupted behind her. "In that case, we'll have to keep you bound.." The voice of the man behind her dripped with evil promise. He yanked her ankle down to lie flush with the wooden leg of the table, the bite of rope pressed against her as he tied her down.

Grace gritted her teeth and closed her eyes. Tears welled and dripped from her chin. She knew they'd take her, there was nothing she could do to stop it but, she would fight them every step of the way. She pulled against the ropes, struggled against the hands holding her down. Someone pressed harder on her shoulders, pinning her down, while another worked on securing her leg. A man shushed her, telling her to be quiet and good and, it would all be over shortly.

Glass shattered somewhere behind her. The men were startled. Gasps and curses were heard as they drew away from the table. Grunts and shouts erupted. The sounds of violence. She rolled off the table. The single candle flickered and died as it was knocked over. Darkness enveloped the room. Sounds of crashing and screams of pain resounded in the house as someone attacked the men. Reaching down, she worked the knot on the rope loose and freed herself. She crawled around blindly, one of the men tripped over her as he too stumbled in the darkness.

Grace located the exit to the rest of the house and scrambled toward it. A hand grasped her arm painfully and she was pulled against a sweaty chest. A cold, sharp blade pressed against her throat. She trembled in terror.

"Move or scream and I'll slit your throat, bitch." The hot, rancid breath of her captor assailed her cheek and her nose. The noise in the room had abated to soft groans. She could clearly hear the *drip, drip, drip* of what was probably blood on the dirty floor and the tell-tale death rattle of a man's last moments of life.

Her heavy breathing and pounding pulse boomed in her ears as her captor sidled around the room, trying to escape.

A fluttering of wings close by caused her captor to startle. "Move and the bitch gets it," he snarled.

Grace remained still in his grip. The blade pressed hard against her throat. She felt the sting as the blade pierced her skin.

"Release her, and I might let you go." The voice from the darkness was strong, confident and masculine.

The man behind her scoffed. "Yeah sure, this bitch is my insurance policy." He held her tighter causing her breath to be expelled with a squeak.

"I will give you only one chance to live." The figure stepped into the dim light filtering through the small, dusty window. She noted the perfect silhouette of a winged man.

Her captor was not intimidated. "I'll take my chances with the bitch."

The winged man appeared to shrug. "So be it."

The winged man melted back into the darkness.

Her captor laughed nervously as he moved through the house, dragging her with him.

"You and I are going to have some fun when we get away from here, sweetheart."

Grace shuddered. The blade remained firmly pressed against her neck and she could feel the dampness of her blood slowly as it trickled over her collarbone. The metallic scent of blood mingled with the rancid scent of his sweat and bad breath. Her stomach churned in rebellion.

Her captor slowed and checked every doorway and hall as they moved through the house. When they reached the front door, he pulled the knife away long enough to reach for the door handle.

A rush of air and a sharp cry from his lips were the only indication he had been attacked.

Grace fell to the floor.

Bright flashes of light, an eruption of ear-splitting gunshots ricocheted off the walls of the small entry hall.

Grace shimmied on her backside to a wall and held her hands over her head as she cowered. The scent of blood hung in the air. Her eyes struggled to focus against the darkness of the house. The ringing in her ears, lessened.

Her gasping, terror filled breaths cut into the deadly silence as she frantically sought the attacker and the man who had captured her. She screeched as the winged figure stood up, towering above her. He stepped closer and leaned down. Strong arms wrapped around her waist and she was whipped over his shoulder.

Feathers tickled her nose. Was her rescuer an Angel or a Demon. Was he really her savior or was he going to finish the job the other bastards had started?

Grace struggled in his firm grip but she was too weak. Hands planted themselves on her naked butt to steady her as he walked down the steps of the abandoned house.

"Put…, put me down, please," she begged. "Your armour is hurting me. Poking me."

He lowered Grace to the ground. When she swayed a little, he placed his hands gently on her arms to hold her steady.

"Are you all right?" His shadowy figure, now cast in the dim light of a crescent moon, revealed his wings were white.

Grace gazed up at him.She was in awe of his handsome features. " "I…, I think so. It feels like I have a small cut where he was holding the knife. She raised her fingers to where her skin stung and felt the wetness of blood. Realizing she was completely naked, she suddenly felt self-conscious. She didn't know why, he would have had a good eyeful of her nude body already. She folded her arms across her breasts, and pressed her thighs tightly together. Yeah, that was going to hide her womanly bits.

"What's your name?" the Angel asked.

"Grace. Yours?"

"Thomas." The Angel smiled..

Her heart flip flopped and her knees weakened.

Thomas sat on the step and pulled her onto his lap giving her time to recover from her ordeal. After a little time had passed, Grace felt stronger.

"I need to go back inside and find something to wear. I can't walk around like this."

"I'll come with you." Thomas stood and carried her back into the house before setting her down on her feet.

She felt steadier now and commenced searching each room for something to wear and anything else that might be useful. An oversized shirt in need of a clean was the only clothing of use she could find. She slipped it on, it covered her body to her knees.

Satisfied, Grace was okay, Thomas set about cleaning the blood and body pieces from his weapon. He was about finished when she returned with a backpack over her arm.

"I found some food and other stuff that might be handy. We can go now." She wanted to be as far away from this hellhole as possible.

Thomas held her hand tightly as they slipped into the darkness of night.

2.

Grace glanced at the Angel. The small camp fire between them cast a flickering glow over their features. The warm light softened him and he looked a little less dangerous than when she had first glimpsed him. She reached inside her backpack and pulled out a tin of preserved meat.

"Sorry I don't have anything fresh. As you know, good food is hard to come by since the war. I'm more than happy to share with you what little I have though."

He smiled at her. "That's fine. You eat what you can. I had already eaten before I came across you and your…. I assume they weren't friends."

"Slavers, they were slavers." Anger laced her voice. She slid the can key into the tiny metal slip and began turning it. The metal parted into a coil.. The salty scent of the meat as it was released made her mouth water. She finished turning the key and the top of the can popped open.

"Mmm, Spam." She eyed the pink and heavily processed meat product that rested on the top of the open can. "Breakfast of champions, so they say." She snorted a wry chuckle as she pulled out her pocket knife and cut a few slices from the rectangular loaf. She picked off a slice and held it between thumb and forefinger before slipping the sweaty, salty slice between her lips.. She chewed thoughtfully.

"So, why is an Angel out here in the Badlands?"She tilted her head toward him. .

"I'm searching for Demons and Angels who want to live in a community where *all* are accepted and wish to live in peace."

Grace watched, fascinated,as he unclipped his armour, allowing it to fall to the ground before shifting out of it. He placed it aside within easy reach, along with his sword. "Humans will be welcomed too, if they are interested." He lay on his side, propped up on an elbow.

"Wow, noble cause. Any takers?"

"No, the Demons seem determined to wreak havoc in the larger cities and the Angels seem happy with their lot in life. The Demons I have come across, appeared to have slipped into insanity and were no longer able to function." He sighed sadly.

"What happened to them?"

"I killed them." Thomas stared into the flames. "It was a mercy, they couldn't be saved."

"How long have you been out here searching?" She could see how the killings affected him and wanted to veer the conversation away from the unpleasantness of what he'd had to do.

"About two months, maybe more." His eyes captured hers and he stared deeply at her.

Grace shifted uncomfortably. His gaze penetrated her deeply, seemingly into her soul.

His eyes, his body, his lush lips; made her feel like a teenager again. Back when she would swoon over her favourite boy band, singer or actor. Those days had been lost in a past when things were far more stable, and the War hadn't happened.

She remembered watching with Ebony and their parents as the ground erupted with Demons and Angels swarmed from the sky to answer the Demon threat. Their parents had not survived that day. The Demons had overpowered the Angels when God and Lucifer had disappeared.

Taking advantage of the confusion and chaos, the two young women were able to escape with their lives. Fires raged on through the days that followed. Their home was burned to the ground, their parents dying as they tried desperately to save it. . Almost everything, everywhere, was lost in the days that followed. Rape gangs appeared and slavers followed shortly after. Anyone unfortunate enough to be caught, was sold to the Demons.

Grace and Ebony were able to escape their city and join a small community. They managed to eke out a living by scavenging what was left in the outer suburbs of the city where the fires had not raged so badly. They lived in an abandoned town, a half-day's travel to the city on foot. A small council helped to keep order and direct their daily lives. It seemed everything had become medieval.

Men roamed the streets with machetes, samurai swords or crossbows, waiting for unsuspecting victims. Guns were in short supply as laws on such weapons before the war had been very tight. With strict controls over guns, people had begun to feel safe again. Until that night when all hell had broken loose and the world had been changed forever.

"Why are you out here on your own?" Thomas noted the faraway look in her eyes.

Grace sighed before taking another slice of spam. "I have to find my sister." Her voice was soft. "She is all I have left in this world."

"Where is she?"

"Slavers have her." She related the story of how their little town had been attacked and their miraculous escape. Tears filled her eyes as she told of how she had witnessed her sister's capture while she scavenged. "I was following them and didn't know that three of them had stayed in the house to scavenge. I had the same idea, and they caught me."

She shuddered at the memory of a sweaty hand being clamped over her mouth. Strong arms worming their way over her body to bring her back against a chest covered in a filthy shirt.

"I need to find some way to save Ebony and the others." She gazed into the fire.

Thomas noted her sadness. "Let me help you. It will be safer with two of us rather than you risking your life and freedom, not to mention that of your sister and friends. You don't know how many men you may encounter."

"You would do that?" Her gaze locked with his and her heart fluttered.

He smiled and nodded. "Yes."

"Why? You don't know me, or my sister, or the people we are with."

"It is the right thing to do. Doing the right thing is expected of Angels."

"No reason other than *It is the right thing to do*?"

"Isn't that the only reason necessary? Get some sleep, I'll keep watch. We'll leave at first light."

Grace nodded and handed him the tin of meat. She watched as he took it with a smile and cut a couple of slices for himself. He replaced the lid to protect the meat from dust and insects, then placed it by the fire to keep it warm for the morning.

Stretching her arms in the air, she yawned and settled down for the night.

Thomas watched as the young woman nestled down on her makeshift bedding to sleep. Her face creased in worry.

His body had responded uncomfortably to her naked state when he had carried her out of the house and away from the men who would have raped and enslaved her.

The Angel's anger at the disgusting state of the human race in these parts bubbled close to the surface. Though it was not unexpected that anarchy would reign supreme. He had known of the Demons overpowering the Angels and humans, effectively taking control of the ruins that survived the war. He had encountered several groups of refugees fleeing or trying to resettle in the lands known as the "Badlands" or "No-man's land."

Her breathing softened as she drifted into sleep. The fire burned low and he banked it to keep it burning through the cooling night, adding a few smaller but stockier pieces of timber that would burn slowly enough to keep them warm.

Alone with his thoughts, Thomas' mind returned to the months after the war. A time before he met Decimus and Eve, for whom he was recruiting - or rather rescuing - Demons and Angels and leading them back to Eve's farm to live peacefully.

His mind wandered to the old church where he had become the Patron Angel.

The giggling of the women in the small meeting room rousing his memory. He lay back naked on the table. The varnish worn in places while the four women stripped their clothes, they had made very quick work of his own. Their gasps of pleasure as they uncovered muscle made him smile. Soft lips met his warm skin. The sensation decidedly erotic as tongues lapped at his tight nipples.

One of the girls moved to the door and locked it, ensuring that they would not be disturbed. Two girls snuggled up on either side of him. Both naked, the globes of their breasts shining in the soft, dim light. Lips met each other, two sets against his one while the other two women took it in turns to bring him to a state of hard, heady arousal. Their tongues stroking his erection. Sometimes in unison, other times separately. He groaned as their warm wet tongues lapped at the hardness between his legs. His hands caressed the soft flesh of the women at his sides, dipping over breasts, hips and into the clefts between their legs.

Soft feminine giggles and moans were his reward as he teased the women at his hands to moan and writhe at his ministrations. Their hands ran over his body, touching his skin and plucking at his nipples. His tongue caressed first one, then the other of the two women who kissed his mouth.

He shifted, moaning as one of the women at his cock slipped her lips over the hardened head, running her tongue over the ridge. Thomas' hand roamed up the bodies of the women, touching, caressing the soft mounds of breasts that came in contact with his calloused fingers. He was pushed back onto the table as the woman who suckled him shifted to mount him. The two women at his lips pulled away as the other who had lavished her tongue over his cock rose to settle herself over his waiting lips. His hands gripped her hips as his tongue moved out and caressed the glistening sex that hovered hot and wet over his mouth. The woman moaned, his moan vibrating through her inner core as the first woman speared herself on him. The two currently unoccupied women turned their attentions to each other. Their lips and hands moving onto their bodies, caressing, groping, licking...

Thomas broke out of his reverie hard and wanted relief. His panting gasps harsh in his ears. His new traveling companion looked at him from her position on the ground. Her dark eyes watched as he regained his composure.

"You ok there?" Grace asked, leaning up on one elbow.

"Yeah, fine." Thomas said, distractedly, "Sorry I woke you."

Grace shook the dirt from her hair, "Couldn't sleep anyway." She said as she reached for the warm spam can and removed the lid. She took out her knife and cut another chunk of the meat. She eyed it before she shoveled it into her mouth and chewed. "You want to get some sleep? I can keep watch."

Thomas nodded, settling down on his side. The dirt crept into his feathers to be shaken out when he got up.

Grace watched over the Angel who had saved her. His face contorted in the dreams which plagued him. His handsome features shadowed in places where the light from the half-moon didn't touch. She stood up quietly and stretched her long limbs out, anxious to get back out and track the slavers. She wanted her sister back, and she would stop at nothing to get her. But, she was also smart. She had barely any combat experience other than survival, and this Angel knew his shit.

She hoped her plan would work.

3.

Thomas' eyes opened to the predawn light and a worn leather boot poking him in the side.

"Hey, time to get up or they'll have too much of a lead on us." Having packed up her gear before she woke him, she kicked earth into the fire to smother the last of the flames.

"Where would they have likely gone?" Thomas asked.

"They'll have headed to the nearest slave trading post. It's unlikely we'll find their tracks if they took the road." Grace shouldered her pack.

Thomas sprang to his feet and shook the dirt from his feathers.

Grace glanced around and pointed in the direction where the trading post was located. "We passed it a day or two ago before I met you." She slipped a pair of sunglasses over her face. "If they want their slaves in good condition to fetch a good price from the Demons and other assholes who want slaves, then they'll have to rest them and feed them." They left their small campsite. Grace peered up at the sky. "We should be there toward the end of the day, hopefully they won't have moved on."

"I could fly you there, it would be much faster."

Grace thought for a moment. Her mind drifting to images of him holding her in his well-muscled arms. The wind flowing over their bodies in flight as he leaned down to press his lips against hers… She shook her head. "Not a good idea. I've been told there are raiders and bandit gangs around here who love nothing more than to shoot at anything flying above their heads."

"But we can catch them so much quicker." Thomas protested.

Grace stopped and turned to face him. "Look. Angel, Demon, eagle, sparrow, it doesn't matter what it is. Most of them are so jacked up on whatever drugs they can get their hands on, or make in their filthy labs, that they can't differentiate between a sparrow and an Angel in flight. Most of the time they look up and can't tell if the wings are black or white." She turned and continued walking, her boots crunching on the dry earth and gravel until she got to the road.

"Ok, no flying then." Thomas followed her.

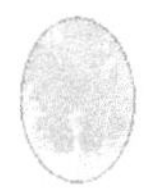

As they walked, Thomas spoke of his friends, Decimus and Eve. Their love had withstood prejudice from humans, and an attempted take-over of her city by the Demon, Marius. Decimus and Thomas had rescued her from Marius, who had been slain by Decimus. They had returned to Eve's home, a large farm away from the city, and begun a sanctuary of sorts for Demons and Angels to live peacefully.

He watched Grace from the corner of his eye. She had the smarts to stay alive and free in this world. The way she listened to his story, but also kept alert to the world around her, made it obvious to Thomas.

"Stop!" She held her hand up in front of him.

"What is it?" Thomas glanced around as his feet skidded on the gravel of the sealed road. He kept himself upright as he came to a stop

"Trouble." She readied her pilfered rifle. The road ahead shimmered with the heat. Figures in the distance twisted in the heated air. "Possibly simple travelers, but more likely slavers." She scooted to the side of the road and hid amongst the dry brush. Thomas followed her, half-drawing his sword from the scabbard.

They waited a few minutes, the sound of clanking chains and sobs of misery reached their ears. The shuffling of booted and bare feet on hot bitumen joined the sounds of misery as men shouted at four slaves.

Three men and a woman were chained and tied in a square two-by-two formation, surrounded by six guards.

Grace scowled and Thomas watched as she pulled back the bolt of the rifle to check the chamber was loaded. She took a deep breath and moved to whisper in his ear.

"I'll take the front, you cover the back. I'm not going to leave the slaves to this fate. No-one deserves this."

Thomas glared back at the shuffling group of miserable slaves and overconfident slavers.

Two held rifles, one a pistol and the others held an assortment of hand weapons, knives, sporting bats, even a tire iron was used to discipline the slaves.

The meaty thump of metal on flesh and the cry of a woman caused Grace's face to darken with rage, and her blood to boil as the adrenalin of her fight response kicked into gear. She jumped to her feet and stepped out in front of the leader of the group.

"You have ten seconds to release them." Grace leveled her weapon.

Raucous laughter answered her demands and the slavers aimed their guns.

"So, you want us to release these degenerate pieces of shit?"

"Yep." Grace held the rifle steady.

The lead slaver scanned the surroundings. "You're all alone out here aren't you? Put the gun down and we might leave you alive long enough to make it to the next town."

"Tobias might like someone with her kind of pluck, Boss."

"Good point. Tobias likes to break the defiant ones."

"Get her." The boss said, keeping his weapon trained on her. The captured slaves cried out as Thomas emerged from behind them. His sword flashed in the sunlight as he cut through the ropes connecting them together.

The three men attacked the slavers from behind while the woman collapsed, sobbing. Thomas continued through the group of people, slicing a slaver's head from his shoulders.

Grace fired her rifle into the stomach of one of the slavers before her. The weapon discharged with an ear-splitting crack, her body jerked with the force, but she held her ground. She watched as the man fell. Crimson blood blossomed like milk in a bowl of water across his lower abdomen as he collapsed back. The expression of disbelief on his face burned itself into Grace's memory as the action around, and before her, slowed. She felt her heartbeat heavy in her chest, her breathing rasping through her open mouth as she watched a man die by her hand. Numbness descended over her body and mind as the reality of what she had done hit her hard.

In her stupor, she didn't notice the leader of the slaver gang raising his rifle to shoot her point blank in the head. A chain whizzed through the air and wrapped itself around the barrel of the gun. The leader was thrown off balance, a shot rang out, the bullet disappeared in a puff of dust in the ground at her feet. Grace was safe.

Using his muscular mass, Thomas barrelled into the leader's skinny frame. His large fists made light work of the man's face while the last of the slavers was taken out by the slaves. Four gunshots cracked out. Each caused Grace to flinch involuntarily before she felt Thomas' hand on her shoulder and his voice soft in her ear.

"Grace, come back to us. Everything is all right, you're safe." Thomas gently removed the weapon from her hand. A single tear slid from her eye to trickle down her cheek. Thomas wiped it away before he lifted her face to his. His heart broke as he gazed into her torture filled eyes..

"I…" she swallowed thickly before forcing the truth from her lips. "I killed him."

Thomas nodded. "Yes. But, he would have killed you, and these people whom he had enslaved would not be free now if it weren't for you. It was incredibly foolish, but what you did was also incredibly brave. You acted at great personal risk." Thomas pulled her to his armored chest. Part of him wishing he could hold her to his skin, feel her warmth against him. Her breath came in sobs as tears cascaded over her cheeks.

The freed slaves gathered boots and clothing from their former captors.

Thomas held Grace until he was sure she had pulled herself together.

The captives approached her. "Thank you." The man's voice betrayed the emotion he felt.

"Is there anything we can do to repay you?" another asked.

"We need information. Do you know if there was a new group of slaves in the trading post, one in particular, a girl named Ebony? She is the sister to Grace here." Thomas said.

Grace explained what her sister looked like, and what she'd been wearing last.

The men thought for a moment but it was the woman who stood up, pain etching lines on her face as she hobbled toward them.

"I remember her. A slaver gang brought her and some other captives past, day before yesterday, I think. They were to be sent for processing to one of the larger settlements. I overheard, they were considered too valuable for the trading post." The woman looked sad. "They were lovely girls, three of them were separated from the main group, including your sister. The others were considered too old for the work of a pleasure slave, but still hardy enough to do manual labor."

The man who had yet to speak stepped forward. "They'll probably take them to the next city over, where the Demon called Maximus will purchase them. He's been buying up all the pretty young women. He wants a harem of pleasure slaves."

Grace felt sick on hearing this news. "I have to get her, I have to free her and the others." She felt Thomas' hand on her shoulder, warmth spreading through the desolate chill in her body. She gazed up at him.

"I'll be with you, every step of the way." His eyes focused on hers, twinkling with determination.

"Thank you." She placed her hand over the top of his and leaned her head to the side to kiss his fingers in gratitude.

They parted from the freed slaves, after helping to clear the road of the dead slavers. The bodies were dragged unceremoniously into the scrub for scavengers to pick clean. Thomas walked beside her, wings slightly outstretched to shield them from the dusty wind and the harsh sunshine beating down on them.

"We'll walk all night if we have to. We will catch up to them." Grace's voice rang with determination.

"Do you know where this larger settlement is? The one after the trading post?"

She scowled and shook her head. "No idea."

"I have an idea that might just work. It could be a way to get information and get your sister and the other girls out of the city.

Grace glanced up at Thomas. "Am I going to like this idea?"

He smiled ruefully. "I'm not sure, probably not."

"I'm *really* not going to like it, am I?"

"I need you to act as my slave."

4.

Grace looked at him as if he'd gone crazy.

"What?"

"You heard me, although you won't actually be my slave, you'll be playing the role of my slave." The expression on her face was priceless.

"Are you serious?" She stopped.

Thomas took a few paces and turned to face her.

"Absolutely." He turned and continued walking, forcing her to jog to catch up with him. "Grace, I have had the undesirable necessity to visit towns and settlements where slavery and slave sales are prevalent. Almost every man, or Demon in the next town has a slave, mostly female. We would blend in better if you were to play the part of my pleasure slave."

Grace sighed. "Can I think about it?"

"Yes, but unless you come up with a better idea, I don't know what else to do."

"You could be my pleasure slave." A grin teased her lips.

Thomas smiled. "Somehow I don't think that would work. I have an excuse for parading you as my slave." He reached back and plucked a black feather from his wings.

"Why is it black?" Grace was confused by the coal-black feather in his fingers.

"I'm almost Fallen." Thomas handed her the feather.

"Fallen?" Grace held the black feather in her fingers. She slowly turned it around,watching as the edges caught the light. "What exactly does that mean?"

"I sinned after the apocalypse. I was on a path of self-destruction. Many Angels Fell alongside me, but I was stopped before I could become what is known as a Fallen."

"What did you do?"

Thomas sighed. "I …" for some reason he couldn't bring himself to tell this beautiful woman before him. "I hurt a lot of people, and I must redeem myself."

Grace waited for him to continue. When no explanation or further information was forthcoming from her companion, she sighed. "We have all done things we are not proud of." She reached over and took his hand, squeezing it before she let it drop.

Thomas glanced at her before turning his face to the far horizon before them.

His hand had felt warm, and Grace found herself wanting more than their brief contact.

The two continued in companionable silence towards the trading post. They passed several travelers, making use of the daylight hours. Some were fortunate enough to have cars or motorbikes still running, if barely. Thick black smoke choked them as one poorly maintained vehicle chugged past them, the engine banging noisily. People moved out of the way as other vehicles passed. One was a small truck with a cattle cage on the back. Cries of misery, human hands and feet protruded through the horizontal bars. A guard with a shotgun sat atop the cab, keeping a vigil over the 'stock'.

Grace watched the truck with concern as it disappeared down the road.

Thomas knew she was wondering if her sister was amongst the miserable humans "There were more males in there than females, and they were all older than you sister." Thomas attempted to comfort her. He placed his arm around her waist and pulled her closer to his side. "We're going to have to find something to make you look more like a pleasure slave, and toting that gun won't help."

"I noticed an abandoned farm a moment ago, there might be something useful there." Grace pointed at a group of buildings in the near distance. A small house and shed were silhouetted against the setting sun.

"Good idea." They left the road and clambered over broken and bent barbed wire fencing. Grace caught her pants on the wire. The tearing of material and her squeak of pain brought Thomas straight to her side. He gathered her up, gently lifted her off the sharp and rusting barbs and set her down on the dried grass on the other side of the fence.

"Are you all right?" His hands caressed her legs to the tear, fingers coming back slightly bloody.

"Yeah, I think it's just a scratch."

Thomas crouched and eased her around, there was a good sized gash on the back of her thigh where the barbed wire had cut

through material and flesh. "This is much more than a scratch."
Thomas gently pressed his fingers against the edges of the gash.
"Maybe there is a first aid kit in the house we can use to clean this
up." Thomas wiped the blood on the skirts of his armor. He took
her hand in his and they hurried through the long grass toward the
farmstead.

His eyes fluttered open, his body a symphony of agony.
Memory flooded back along with the clearing of his blurry vision.
The slaves had escaped, with the help of some attractive young
woman, and an Angel. His boss and the other men who worked
with him lay dead in a ditch. Jackson, a sick fuck with a penchant
for kids, was lying across his torso, making it difficult to breathe.
The dead weight of the cold body and the stench of blood and
bodily fluids released upon death were mere distractions to his
simmering rage.

With a grunt he shoved Jackson off his body. The fucker's
demise was no loss to anyone, but losing the boss was something
he *could* be pleased about. In the grand scheme of things, it meant
a promotion of sorts. But first things first. Revenge. He scrounged
what little was left on the bodies of the others before hauling
himself out of the ditch to the main road.

His body ached, his muscles bruised and swollen where the
slaves had bashed him with their chains. Those he would hunt
down and deal with in good time, but right now, he had a great
desire to find and capture a certain girl, and kill her Angel
companion.

She would be his new toy, and she would regret the day she crossed Franklin Goode.

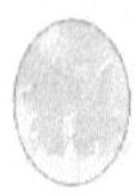

Grace hissed through her teeth at the pain.

Thomas glanced at her sympathetically. "I'm sorry, I know it hurts but we have to clean it. We can't risk it becoming infected." He poured more vodka over the wound.

"I can do this myself you know, and do we need my jeans pulled down this far?"

"I've seen you naked, and trust me, if we're going to be able to carry off this plan of mine, you'll be wearing a *lot* less than you are now."

Grace pushed herself up onto her elbows from her face down position on the table.

"Exactly how much less are we talking about?" She glared back at him.

"Lay down." Thomas said, pressing his hand against her shoulder until she complied. He wet a scrap of cloth with the vodka again before he applied it to her wound. "You'll be wearing a bra and panties, G-string preferred." He dabbed the cloth against the cut and heard the hissing intake of her breath as the alcohol stung the raw and exposed nerves.

"G-string! Oh God, anything but that."

"I've heard they can be quite comfortable." Thomas chuckled.

"Really? Are *you* wearing one?" Her question met with silence but he paused in his ministrations. "Didn't think so. Who in their right mind would want a string up their ass?"

Thomas tapped her on the shoulder twice and she took it as her cue to sit up. With her legs dangling over the table, he took the strip of an old linen sheet they had cut and wrapped it around her leg.

Thomas took hold of her waist, as she sat up, he gazed into her eyes. Pools of beautiful clear green stared back at him. He was enthralled, enchanted, totally enamoured by their depths. His hands moved to her back, supporting her, holding her. "Are you sure you're ok with doing this? There may be some…" He paused, trying to think of the right words. "…situations where we have to prove you are my pleasure slave."

Grace gazed back at him, her eyes locked with his. Her heart beat faster as his hands feathered up her back, their warmth radiating into her skin. Her voice was soft when she spoke. "Then, maybe we should practice. You know, to get comfortable with touching each other."

Thomas chuckled softly. "I'm touching you now, and you seem pretty comfortable with it."

She moved her hands up his chest over the singlet top he wore after changing out of his armour into something more comfortable.. The feel of her light fingers sending sweet shivers through his chest down to his groin.

"Yes, but what if we need to kiss in front of someone?"

The room heated, the atmosphere thick, more electric between them.

"Kiss? Yes, we should definitely practice kissing." He leaned in and gently brushed his lips over hers.

They both flinched as a feeling like a jolt of electricity zapped its way through each of their bodies.

Grace pressed herself against the hard muscle of his chest, her arms snaked around his shoulders. Her lips parted and she invited him to taste her.

Thomas accepted the invitation, his tongue tempting hers to play as he took command of their *practice*.

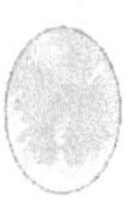

Grace melted against him, letting herself go completely. Her body begged, demanded that she submit to him.

Thomas kneed her legs apart and moved closer into her. He ran his hands over the buttons of her jacket. Deft fingers plucked them open. With his help, she shrugged out of the cumbersome clothing. Her lips pressed hard to his and her eyes closed when she heard the jacket drop to the floor.

Thomas pulled away from her. His breathing matched hers in heavy, lustful pants. She kicked off her boots followed by her jeans while he disposed of his singlet top. He discarded it at his feet with her clothing before kicking it all aside and moving back into her. His gaze radiated lust matching her own.

Their lips crushed together, hands roamed over each other's bodies as gasps and moans slipped from parted lips. Thomas' hands slipped under her shirt to find her breasts encased in a lacy bra. He found the clip at the front and freed them from their satin-and-lace prison.

Thomas reveled in the feel of the soft, warm mounds in his hands. His cock strained against his jeans as Grace arched into his caressing touch. Leaning back, she granted him full access before she slipped her shirt off, dropped it to the floor, and wrapped her legs around him. Squeezing his ass with her feet, she drew him closer. Her pussy clashing with the impressive bulge in his pants.

"Kissing's good," she said breathlessly. "But what if we have to do other things?"

Thomas kissed the nape of her neck, feathered light kisses to her collarbone, alternating his words with each touch. "Other. Things. Like. What?"

Grace slipped her hands inside the waistband of his jeans. It was all he could take. Within seconds, Thomas had his jeans unzipped and sliding off. His cock sprang free, erect and proud.

"Commando, huh?." Grace smiled as she traced a finger over the head of his cock and along the shaft.

Thomas tilted his head back, closed his eyes and moaned.

"I'm glad we're doing this. I might have blown our cover if I had unsuspectingly come across this monster." Grace stroked him.

Thomas gripped her shoulders and lay her back down on the table.

"Grace," he whispered into her hair as he kissed her temple. He reached down and ripped away her panties with a satisfying tearing sound.

"Hey, I need those!"

He loomed over her, straddling her with his legs and caging her in with muscular arms. "No, you don't." He shifted to take one of her hardened nipples into his mouth. His fingers played between the moistening lips of her pussy.

Grace gasped and writhed as he teased her folds. "You're right. I *definitely* don't need them."

Thomas' fingers teased her into submission. He hungered for her. He wanted her. Needed her. His mind rebelled against his body, and visions of black feathers ran through his mind's eye. He shoved the thoughts of *falling* away as he made love to the strong and brave woman beneath him. His tongue trailed down her skin to the sweet place between her thighs. Grace cried out as he flicked her clit, while thrusting two fingers into her pussy.

He removed his fingers, slick with her juices and slipped them between his lips, licking them clean before he moved atop her, mounting her. The head of his cock pressed against her damp folds. She gazed up at him as his searched her face for any signs of regret. He found only want. In his eyes she was perfection. He smiled at her, hoping his eyes showed the emotion he felt for her. He had known her for only a few days, and already he felt the strength of his emotions drawing him to her.

He groaned as he thrust into her. Her body responded to his every touch, his kisses, his body as he claimed her. Making love to Grace was nothing like his near-falling. This woman was different. He felt in his heart, she was different. Her hands wrapped around his body, holding him close as he moved within her. For the first time, he gave pleasure. In the past he'd taken from many other women in the church where he was Patron Angel.

Grace moaned and jerked beneath him. Her body was a temple, the goddess beneath him deserved to be worshiped, loved and cherished. For the briefest of moments, he wondered what would happen when they found her sister.

He knew time was of the essence, but this, this was more than a pleasant distraction. Grace needed him and he needed her. She cried out as her rapturous climax slammed into her. The spasms of her core pushed him over the edge and his seed spilled inside her. She shivered beneath him with the aftershocks of her orgasm, her body covered in a light sheen of sweat. He pulled out of her, reached down to the floor and snagged his singlet.

With loving care, he cleaned her up. Thomas wiped the sweat from her breasts, stomach and the trail of cum from her inner thighs. She lay quietly, breathing heavily.

"Thomas."

"Yes, sweetheart."

"You can practice with me anytime."

Thomas stood and leaned over her. He placed a gentle kiss to her lips. "Likewise. Come, we have to leave soon if we want to get to the trading post before sundown."

Grace bounced to her feet, her clothing covered her body in a heartbeat. "I'll have a quick look around to see if there's anything we can scrounge to trade. And, I hope I have a clean pair of panties in my bag." She winked before heading off to explore.

"Good idea, I'll look in the sheds for some chains."

5.

Grace moved around the kitchen, finding cans and packages of dried foods. She loaded as much as she could carry into a bag.

Thomas appeared in the doorway with a spiked, black leather collar, as thick as her index finger was long, and a leather leash. "This was all I could find, I think whoever lived here used to fight dogs. There was a small pit in one of the sheds and a lot of dried blood." He held the leash and collar out to Grace.

"This is new." She ran her hand over the shiny metal spikes, and tugged the price tag off, the string broke with a snap.

"There were others, but I wouldn't put them around your neck." He hoped she wouldn't discover he was hiding something. He had found the pit, several dead dogs and men with gunshot wounds to their heads. The stench of death had been overpowering. He was grateful the animals no longer suffered and their tormentors had received a just end. He'd searched through a cupboard and found the collar, still with its tag on it, and a leash. He left, shutting the door on the grisly scene.

They left the farm with their hands clasped firmly together, fingers intertwined. Thomas noticed a glow about Grace as they walked. Her hair was a little more disheveled, and she moved with a slight limp due to the gash on her leg. They stopped a few miles from the trading post to check on the wound. Thomas placed the collar around Grace's neck and attached the leash. He caressed her face and kissed her gently.

"It won't be for long, I promise." He'd noticed the dismal expression on her face as the leather touched her skin, and the leash was attached.

She nodded. "I know. We have to do this, or else we'll never find Ebony."

Thomas stopped and turned her to face him. "You are very brave, sweetheart. I admire your courage. He leaned down, gathered her into his arms and kissed her.

"Now just remember, you have to play the part of my slave." He walked onward, looking for other people on the road.

Grace followed. "I'll try, but I need to find her."

"We just need to get directions to the city where Maximus rules."

Grace frowned at Thomas's scowling face. "You know him?"

"I've heard of him, though it was nothing good." Thomas checked his armor and sword at his hip. "He was one of the most stable survivors of the war, and quickly got his men back under control. He slaughtered hundreds of Angels and Humans, taking over the city in a matter of hours." Thomas studied the area as the ramshackle fence and gates of the trading post came into view. He clutched the leash tighter in his hand, pulling her closer to him. "Lower your head, sweetness, it's time to play slave."

Grace nodded and lowered her head, her eyes quickly darting around before they arrived at the gates.

Armed sentries waited atop crudely constructed towers above the gates while other guards waited at the gates themselves. Thomas approached the first guard.

"Here to trade?" The guard cast a lustful eye over Grace.

Thomas' hands curled into fists as his blood boiled and rage welled. "Yes. I have this useless thing and some other goods."

The guard approached and studied Grace closer. He grabbed her chin, pulling her head left and right, up and down before he walked around her, patting her down and groping her ass. She held up well to the guard's inspection. Thomas swallowed a smile. He could tell she wanted to slap the bastard into the next millennium.

"A good specimen, isn't she? It's a pity I have to rid myself of her, but she can be troublesome at times."

The guard grunted.

Grace flinched as he ran his hand over the wounded leg.

"She's got a wound here?" The man looked enquiringly at Thomas, his hand remained on her leg. The guard squeezed the injured leg, causing Grace to squeak in pain.

"Yes, stupid bitch thought she could run from me and got herself hurt."

"That will lower her price."

"Yes, I know. Are you going to allow us inside or not?" Thomas was becoming impatient.

"The market doesn't usually take injured stock. Sales masters prefer their stock to be intact." The guard moved closer to Thomas.

Thomas raised his hand, beckoning Grace to his side. She moved quickly, handing him the bag with their scavenged supplies.

Thomas reached into the bag and pulled out several tins of food and packets of instant noodles. The guard examined the bribe and nodded. "Welcome to Market Town, where everything is for sale for the right price."

Thomas nodded and thanked the guard. The gates swung open with a horrendous screeching of metal-on-metal, revealing the secondary gates where he had to offer another bribe to the next guard to get into the town proper.

Grace rolled her eyes and sighed, earning her a cuff to the back of the head from Thomas. "Behave woman, I'll be free of your nonsense soon enough, but until then, you are still my slave." The eyes watching them from the shadows moved quickly to report the arrival of an Angel.

The bar was dingy, cobbled together with corrugated iron, and a small caravan which served drinks and tinned foods through a broken window. Music blared from an old jukebox, powered by solar panels jury-rigged to the roof and connected to old car batteries. Scantily clad women with chain collars around their necks served drinks and serviced customers at their seats. Naked women danced in time to the raucous music on a stage made of wooden pallets.

Thomas sat at a table and pulled Grace onto his lap. He absently stroked her back with his hand as she leaned against the hard chest plate of his armor. He scanned the bar, looking for someone who might be able to offer them some information on the best or safest route to Maximus' city. He knew Grace would be doing the same.

A drunk stumbled against their table and leered at Grace. "When you're done with her, can I have her?" His breath was rancid with alcohol, old food and rotting teeth.

Grace tried not to gag.

Thomas held her tighter to him. "No, this one is mine." He glared at the drunk until he got the message and stumbled off, groping a passing bar slave as he went. The slave approached their table to take their order.

"Directions, to the city controlled by Maximus." Thomas said, answering her question of "what's your pleasure?"

The girl glanced about, a frantic expression crossed her face. "I'm sorry sir, I can only serve you drinks, food, or other pleasures available here." She ran her hands over barely covered breasts. "I'm sure your pleasure slave wouldn't mind if I joined in the fun as well?" She smiled revealing missing teeth. Her bloodshot eyes revealed the abuse of drugs rampant amongst the population here. Grace elbowed his ribs. Thomas shook his head.

"Where can I get the information I seek?" Thomas persisted. His hand moved to caress Grace's breasts through the thin shirt she wore. He knew eyes were watching them, appearances must be upheld. But, damn if he wasn't feeling the effects of his hands on her body. She shifted a little on his lap, not helping his predicament. Grinding her ass against his erection almost caused him to groan in sexual frustration.

His mind drifted to a desire of throwing Grace onto the table, ripping her clothes from her body and pounding into her until they both reached their delicious climaxes while the whole bar watched. He shook the wickedly erotic thoughts from his mind. They would need to find somewhere private so he could relieve his sexual tension. He reached a hand to her ass and gripped it.

"I'd suggest you ask the mayor of Market Town, Tobias. Maximus' City is well protected and unless you have the right pass phrase for the day, or a pass from Tobias or Maximus themselves, you don't get in."

Thomas nodded and thanked the slave. He handed her a packet of noodles for her snippet of information. Food and other useful goods seemed to be the normal payments as coin and money were no longer useful currency.

They left the dingy bar and strolled around. Lodging for the evening was proving problematic. 'No Vacancy' signs adorned all of the hovels which masqueraded as accommodation.

Thomas led Grace along another street, and they were stopped by a large group of men.

Grace turned and looked behind them, another group of men blocked their retreat.

They were trapped.

One of the men stepped forward into the dim light cast by a small flickering light bulb. "Tobias would like to see you." He smirked as he lit a cigar and nodded a signal to the men behind them.

Darkness came over them as sacks were thrown over their heads, and they were bound at the wrists.

6.

The stench of musty material assailed their senses as they were bullied blindly through the streets. The occasional shattering of a bottle echoed loudly accompanied by feminine screams, masculine shouts and running feet. Grace wriggled her wrists, trying to find a more comfortable position as pins and needles flowed through her nerves.

They walked for about twenty minutes before they were forced to stop. Doors opened and they were pushed forward. The change in atmosphere was sudden. From the chill of the exposed night, to the warmth of a building filled with people. Soft voices, gasps, groans, moans and an occasional cry of rapture were heard as they walked.

They were stopped, their hoods removed. Grace squinted in the sudden brightness of the room, which in effect was due to the darkness she and Thomas had been subjected to. The reality of the room shocked her. Candles of red, white and black burned on shelves and in candelabras. Their multi-coloured wax forming colourful stalactites as the hot wax dripped down and cooled.

Around them were couples and ménages. Men, women, joined in undulating, writhing forms. The stench of sweat and sex permeated everything and the humidity made Grace's body damp with her own sweat. Thomas stood beside her, proud and upright, his bound hands covering his groin. She wondered if all the sex in the room was affecting him. Her mind shot back to the memory of their own coupling and her body responded.

Her attention was diverted to the dais which rose before them. A large, shadowy figure reclined on a divan. Wings sat relaxed against his back, and he held a naked blonde woman in his arms. His hands stroked her breasts and stomach down to her mons. The woman arched into his touch like a cat, stretching her supple body, and making the heavy chain attached to her collar clink as she moved. He was silent for a few minutes while he played with his 'pet'.

Their host turned his eyes from the lithe young woman in his arms to gaze upon his guests.

"Greetings, I am Tobias." He said, his voice hard and gravelly. He stroked the woman again, her moans soft, almost lost among the other sounds of pleasure.

"What brings an Angel and his slave to my town?" he shifted slightly, resting on one elbow. He indicated for a naked slave to bring him refreshments. He took a glass of wine in his hand before caressing the breast of the serving slave. Grace's face flushed and she lowered her gaze. This was wasting time, they had to get out of here before it was too late to save her sister from whatever damned fate awaited her with the Demon Maximus.

Thomas stepped forward. "My name is Thomas. I seek permission to go to the City where Maximus resides." He bowed his head respectfully.

"Why would you wish that? Do you wish to offer your services as a whore to the Demon Maximus? Or do you wish to offer him your pretty little slave?" Tobias shoved the girl on his divan to the floor. She scrambled to the side as he rose to his feet.

He wore a *Greco-Roman* style toga, his wings shining black. Several white feathers interrupted the perfection.

Thomas remained silent, but Grace knew his mind would be assessing everything that was happening. He would be trying to figure out the best way to get them both out of here alive, unmolested, and un-enslaved by Tobias. On their way to save Ebony.

Thomas regarded the Fallen before him, this one was beyond redemption and he didn't seem to care.

"I seek to purchase this one's sister. She, along with this slave, was promised, but stolen from me." He stayed alert as Tobias walked around the pair. He reached out and caressed Grace's ass through the material of her shorts.

"She is not dressed appropriately for a pleasure slave." Tobias ran his hands over Grace's back.

She couldn't stop herself from shivering in fear and revulsion as Tobias's hands reached up into the tresses of her hair, gripped the strands in his fist and wrenched her head back. He trailed a finger over the brand new collar around her neck while his eyes searched hers. Defiance burned in her before she looked away.

Tobias grinned before he released her and turned to face Thomas.

"We have just arrived from the road. Her attire is more fitting for travel rather than what you would deem appropriate for one of her station. I was forced to bring her along as I refused to leave her behind at the mercy of my other servants. She and her sister are very,… special to me." Thomas lifted his chin and fought the urge to rip Tobias' head off for touching Grace.

"We shall see she is now dressed as befits her station." Tobias walked slowly past Thomas, his hand trailing along the wings. Lightly fingering the black feathers and caressing the tips. Thomas shivered at his touch, and was disgusted to find, it elicited a sensual feeling through his body.

Tobias summoned two nearby slaves. "Take her, have her cleaned up and dressed properly for the evening meal. My Fallen brother shall be my guest tonight."

Grace was grabbed by the two naked slave girls and hauled off, she struggled a little before a look from Thomas stilled her and she complied.

Tobias returned to his divan and dragged a dark haired slave to her knees to crawl before him. He set her between his legs and pushed her face to his crotch. She lifted the skirts of his toga and began to caress and lick his cock. He stroked her hair as she worked on him.

"Refresh yourself, my friend, I'll have your pet brought to you." Tobias moaned softly as the girl worked him. He flicked his hand to his guards, who untied Thomas and led him in the opposite direction from where the slave girls had taken Grace.

His heart beat wildly in his chest. His brow furrowed in worry for her.

One of the guards noticed and smirked. "Don't worry about your whore. She's off limits to the rest of us. Don't be surprised if Tobias insists on a taste of her delights." Another guard sniggered.

Thomas scowled at the fool. It was tempting for the powerful Angel to reach out and snap his neck, end his miserable life, but it was not worth another black feather.

He was escorted to an opulent room in which stood a large four poster bed with looped leather strips attached to each post. Two pleasure slaves awaited him, their sheer clothing leaving little-to-nothing to the imagination. Their soft hands took his and led him to the bed where he sat down heavily on the soft covers.

The slaves removed his clothing, their eyes alight at the muscles of his chest. Their hands and tongues caressed his pectorals and he felt himself harden with their attentions. But, it felt *wrong*.

Before Grace, before he knew Decimus and Eve, he would have been all over these two beautiful women like a fire to petrol-soaked dry grass on a hot and windy day.

Now, he felt dirty. He had seen what he could have become had he let his lust and greed take over. Had he fallen completely, he would be not unlike Tobias.

Thomas pushed the slaves from him. They fell to their knees.

"Do we displease you, master?" one asked shyly.

"No, no." Thomas dragged his fingers through his hair.

"You prefer men?" the other slave asked. "We can have one of the male slaves brought up if you prefer."

"No. I do not sleep with men." Thomas gazed at the two women before him. "I would like a bath, but with my own slave attending me." The two women nodded and stood. They slipped from the room leaving Thomas to wait.

His mind wandered to the evening ahead, he would have to stay alert. Tobias was a dangerous Fallen. Grace and his parts would have to be played well.

A knock at the door startled him from his thoughts. Grace was escorted in, wearing a black satin wrap. The guards left her standing before Thomas, her eyes downcast, playing a slave almost to perfection.

As soon as the door closed, he stood and embraced her. The scent of lavender and rose wafted from the warmth of her skin. She had been bathed and dressed, her hair brushed .She was a vision of loveliness.

"Are you all right?" He pressed his lips to her temple, before pulling away. Lifting her chin with two fingers, he gazed into her eyes.

"I'm fine."

Thomas bent forward and kissed her. His hands moved over her shoulders, taking the satin robe from her body to reveal a black teddy. The garment was made of strips of satin, strategically covering her breasts and mons, with black lace covering the rest of her skin. Seeing her in this made him hard again. His lips touched her jawline, moving down her neck. He got down on bended knee, caressing her as he began to explore her body with trembling fingers and lips.

Thomas located a hardened nipple under the material and sucked it into his mouth. Grace moaned and tilted her head back, pressing herself against his body, her hands holding his head against her breast while he suckled her through the material.

His hands worked at the knotted material holding the robe to her body. It slipped to the floor without a sound. Thomas ran a hand up her thigh. The long limb had been cleared of hair.

He trailed his nimble fingers to her pussy, finding it also clear of the usual dark curls. She flinched a little. "Are you all right?"

"It's a little tender down there from the waxing."

Thomas smiled, and stood, sweeping an arm under her legs, he carried her to the bed. He lay her down on the soft covers before he hiked up the hem of the teddy, revealing her beautiful womanhood. It was a delightful shade of pink from the waxing. He gently stroked the area, soothing her with his fingers before he moved to kiss her there.

Grace moaned softly as Thomas' tongue darted out to taste her, swiping between her bare lips and delving into her slit. She gasped and writhed. His strong hands holding her in place. She'd never felt so deliciously helpless, and she loved it.

He slipped two fingers into her damp cunt and began to slowly tease her, finding her g-spot and making her wetter. She gasped and moaned loudly. Thomas pulled back, her moan of disappointment harsh in his ears.

"I'll be back, my sweet. I need to get rid of my jeans."

Grace propped herself up on her elbows, watching him strip while she lay naked and wanting on the bed.

Thomas smiled at her as he removed his pants. His cock, freed from his pants, jutted out proudly. A shining bead of pre-cum glistening on the tip.

Grace lowered herself back onto the bed as Thomas moved over her and leaned in for a kiss. His lips met no resistance as she caressed his face, drawing him closer to her. He gripped his hard shaft and pressed it against her entrance, sliding along her lips, pressing the tip against her clit and rubbing his cock in small circles against the sensitive nub.

Grace gasped as she felt him press harder against her, a moan escaping her lips as he penetrated her deeply in one smooth thrust. She arched her back with each hard thrust he gave her, her beautiful voice crying out as pounded her into the mattress. Her hands moved across Thomas's back, her fingernails digging in as she rushed toward climax. Her body trembled as she felt the exquisite pleasure building to a point where she could no longer contain it. She screamed when he reached down and stroked her clit with a finger, reaching deeply to roar out his own climax as her sheath tightened around him.

Thomas shuddered his release and collapsed onto the bed beside her, pulling her close and kissing her softly.

"I'll never use you like Tobias uses those women." His voice conveyed the sincerity of his promise.

Grace breathed heavily, her body covered in a light sheen of sweat. "I know." She rolled over in his arms to face him. His deep eyes studied her as she smiled and placed a hand to his cheek. "I don't know what will happen to us after we rescue Ebony."

"Don't think about it until the time comes. We'll work something out." Thomas held her close.

Grace nodded. "We've got an hour until our 'host' will want us to join him for dinner." Grace rose reluctantly. Her body glowed with the satisfaction of sex.

Thomas followed her into the bathroom, where she ran hot water into a bath. He hardened again as she bent over the tub to turn the faucets on. He moved behind her and pressed his erection against the slick folds of her pussy.

"Grace, I… I need you again." An overwhelming urge to take her gripped him.

She gasped as he entered her. His energetic pumping as she leaned over the bath, caused her full breasts to swing in time with the hard thrusts.

Her hands gripped the side of the tub as the hot water flowed, steaming the bathroom. When the water neared a point where she knew it would overflow with both of them in the tub, she reached over and turned off the taps.

Thomas moaned as he thrust within her. He felt his balls tighten, grabbed Grace's shoulders and lifted her up. He held her back against his chest, one hand rubbing against her clit with his thumb, the other hand pressed against her breasts.

Grace cried out as her orgasm rocked through her body, her feet dangled off the ground as Thomas held her. His motions finally slowed as he hit his peak, his hot seed jetting into her as he groaned, trembling within her warmth.

She breathed hard as he placed her gently to her feet. Planting kisses along her back. "Sorry, you just…" His breath was eratic, he was lost for words.

Grace turned to him with a smile of a well-satisfied woman. "No need to apologize."

She helped him into the bath, taking up a cloth and slipping in behind him. She washed his back as he relaxed in the warmth of the bath. His hands ran along her legs, massaging the muscles. The crude bandage had been removed from her leg while under the care of the other slaves and replaced with a clean, waterproof medical strip.

Bathed, well serviced and refreshed, Thomas and Grace dried each other and dressed, preparing for their evening meal with Tobias.

7.

Grace stood, chained and collared, two steps behind Thomas as they waited at the grand looking table. It was spread with *real* food and Grace felt her stomach rumbling. Thomas tightened his grip on the chain, making it jingle. Grace stiffened her posture, lowering her head slightly. Her body language almost perfect for a slave.

Candles flickered in silver candelabras, casting an eerie glow over the spread. The scent of hot, melting wax drifted through the room, mingling with the scents of roasted meats, vegetables and fine gourmet sauces.

Their host entered leading two of his naked slave girls on chains. He sat at the head of the table and summoned Thomas over. Grace felt the slack in the chain tighten and she followed Thomas to his seat. Tobias' two girls sat on the floor, one on either side of his chair. Thomas tugged on Grace's chain. She took the hint and knelt down immediately beside him. He stroked her hair. "Good girl."

He turned his full attention to Tobias. "I'd like to thank you for your hospitality tonight Tobias."

More slaves entered and began pouring red wine into crystal classes.

Tobias took his filled glass and raised it to Thomas. "No, my friend. It is you whom I wish to thank, for I hardly get to spend any time with a fellow Angel, let alone a fallen brother." He smiled but it didn't quite reach his eyes which flickered to the far corner of the room where figures hid in the shadows.

"My friend, I understand your concern and the need for security, but I am here unarmed. I would never threaten a host." Thomas sipped at the wine.

Grace glanced up at him, concern in her eyes. he noticed her look and placed a reassuring hand on her head, petting her as he would a pet dog.

"You cannot be too careful these days." Tobias nodding to his slaves to begin serving. The two women stood gracefully and began to select foods for their master and his guest, serving them both on silver platters.

Tobias pulled one of his slaves to his lap, before sending the other girl away. The girl began to hand feed her master.

Thomas tugged on Grace's chain. She stood and he pulled her into his lap. She glanced at the platter of food, and then to the girl and Tobias. She took up a fork and speared roasted chicken before turning to feed Thomas. He took the meat from her hand gently, chewing and swallowing. His eyes remained on hers. He knew they needed to leave as soon as possible, but they were still in a precarious position. To have the truth discovered would be devastating to their cause.

"So, when did you need to be at Maximus' city?" Tobias asked around a mouthful of food. His slave lapped at a drop of gravy at the corner of his mouth with her tongue. Tobias' hand ran up and down her back, while his free hand caressed her generous breasts.

"As soon as possible. I would prefer to claim this girl before any there have tasted her. I will still have her as my own even if she has been sullied, but I prefer to have my slaves untouched by any other."

Tobias grinned. "I understand." He picked up his glass and finished his wine. The slave girl offered him another morsel, he took half of the meat in his mouth and then leaned forward. She licked her lips and took the offered piece from his lips. She chewed quickly then thanked her master with a seductive kiss. Grace could see the large bulge under his robes.

Tobias roughly grabbed the slave and turned her so her back faced him. He positioned her and she moaned softly. Grace lowered her eyes, knowing Tobias had penetrated her. He thrust up into the girl with no consideration for the fact they were at the dinner table.

Beneath her, Grace felt Thomas harden. Her face heated and she struggled to ignore the sudden need between her thighs. Thomas pressed harder and harder against her ass.

"I think we can arrange for you to enter Maximus' city, but you will need to get there yourself, we cannot spare any vehicles. I will have a scribe write the letter tonight, you may leave first thing in the morning, with my blessings." On his lap the girl gasped and moaned. He slapped her on the ass. "Silence, whore. Your master is speaking with a guest. He thrust up hard into the slave, and she gripped the edges of the table.

"Forgive me, master. This slave offers her apologies."

Tobias nodded, leaning in to bite the nape of her neck. "I will punish you thoroughly, later." He grunted as he thrust harder into her.

Grace finished feeding Thomas the last food on the platter. He leaned back in the chair, pulling her against his chest. Her angel stroked her back gently, his hand soothing her trembling body.

"So, tell me, how did you come to be in this place? Thomas asked.

Tobias grunted one last time and pushed his slave from his lap.

"Clean me, whore." She dropped to her hands and knees and began to lick him clean. He turned his attention back to his guest.

"Well, after the war, when the Lord and the Devil abandoned us here, I decided there was no point in being pious, at least not on earth. What was the point?" He pushed the girl's head further down over his cock. "I worked with a few Demons, including Maximus, who took over the city where we had once fought against each other. He seemed to have the right ideas about us all working together. The Humans were the ones who should bow to *us*, as the superior beings. It is up to *us* to lead them." He closed his eyes for a moment while the girl's head bobbed up and down in his lap.

"He brought many of our insensate brother's together, both Angel and Demon." He shook his blackened feathers out, stretching the wings slightly as if he was uncomfortable. "I took in slaves, many beautiful women, offering them as gifts to Maximus, who offered me the position of leader of this little ramshackle trading post. This building was one of the few to remain intact. It was the town hall. I don't think anyone remembers the name of this town, not that it matters. Many of the records were burned with the rest of the place after the war." He pushed away the slave who had finished cleaning him. She took up her original position on her knees at his feet.

Thomas continued to stroke Grace's back softly. He could feel her trembling slightly, either from anger, fear or perhaps, closer to the truth, a bit of both.

"And you?" Tobias asked him. "Your story?"

"Mine?" Thomas spoke hesitantly, knowing he hadn't told Grace everything yet. He tensed slightly, but knew he would have to recount it sooner or later.

"I first began my fall when I was seduced by a minister's daughter. I was the Patron Angel of her father's parish. I fucked many women from the congregation after that. Bible study, religious discussions, all were a front for me to fuck my way through their numbers, sometimes with more than one woman at a time." Thomas sipped at the last of his wine as his mind drifted to the past.

"It came to an abrupt halt when the men of the town and parish realized what was going on. The daughter of the mayor was in my bed, riding me hard when they came for me. She was shot and killed by her own brother, his gun went off before he knew it was her. She died in my arms, and I descended into a battle rage. I slaughtered those who came against me and injured many others in my escape." Thomas remained silent for a moment. His mind drifted to the past images. The blood on his hands, the look of shock on Jacinta's face as the bullet entered her back, pierced her heart and exploded out of her chest. His face and torso had been spattered with her blood and shattered organs.

Thomas shifted his thoughts away from that horrendous day, when his falling had almost been completed, to the present. A lie would be required, it would be another strike against him in his falling. Another black feather would appear. One step closer to true fallen status, and his wings would be as dark as Tobias', with only a tiny scattering of white.

"I wandered for days in a daze before I found this tasty morsel." Thomas gripped Grace's chin, striking a finger along her jawline before his lips pressed against the places where his fingers had been seconds before. "She was wandering the roads, searching for her sister, who had been taken by a group of Slavers. The same group who had promised me both girls and swindled me by letting them both get away. So you can imagine my joy when I picked her up with a promise of finding her sister, but I think she realizes now, she and her sister will not escape me." Thomas grinned wickedly and gripped the chain around her neck.

"You… you *lied* to me?" Grace's voice broke as she cried out.

"My dear, you should never have trusted me in the first place." Thomas smiled at her, there was no way he could wink at her, to make sure she understood he was only playing a part. The betrayal she felt was clear in her eyes. He gripped her chin and smiled. "I am a Fallen, my dear. We are as trustworthy as any human here. That is to say… not at all. I will not release you after we leave, this was not a *pretend* thing to try to get your sister back for you. If she is anything like you, then I will want to have her for myself, and as well as you."

Tobias smiled, his hands clasped together before his face as his elbows rested on the table. "My dear Thomas, what a lovely way to betray the trust of someone." He laughed. "She thought you were pretending to help her?" He laughed again as Thomas glanced toward him and nodded.

Grace struggled in his grip, trying to free herself from him. He quickly wrapped the chain around her. She shrieked and clawed at him until he had her bound. She struggled for a few minutes more before she relented, tears running down her face as soft sobs took over.

Thomas looked to Tobias. "Would Maximus consider taking me on as part of his organisation? I'm looking for a place in this world to settle down, especially when I get this one's sister in my clutches." Thomas grinned

"There is always a place for a fellow Fallen in Maximus' court, I'll let him know you are trustworthy amongst your own kind. I'm sure he'll find something for you." Tobias rose and Thomas following suit. "Rest for the evening. I will have my scribe bring the papers to you and you may depart for Maximus' city in the morning. You will be given directions then." Tobias nodded to his guest, indicating he could take his leave.

Thomas smiled, and pulled a stunned and numbed Grace from the room.

A man, Goode, hobbled from the shadows toward Tobias.

"Was that them?" the Fallen Angel asked.

"Yes, she shot Grubb and he slaughtered two of your men. The slaves took out the rest after he'd freed them." Goode snarled. "I want her. I want her to feel the fear and the pain she deserves. I want to punish her for killing my brother."

Tobias placed his hand on the angry man. "I will grant you ownership of her, if you capture her, but you must kill him first. And, I want first taste of the goods when you bring her back. There is to be no fucking her on the way here."

Franklin Goode nodded his agreement. "We will get them out on the road, no-one will come to their aid. It will be quick and dirty."

"Good, just the way I like it." Tobias smirked. He would have that delightful little whore Thomas seemed determoned to protect. He could smell her scent. She aroused him like no other and he would not be satisfied until he had a taste. Perhaps he would even keep her, eliminate Goode from the picture entirely. There were a few circles which would take male slaves to fight in the blood-sport arenas which had cropped up since the war. Goode would make an excellent blood-slave.

Tobias smiled as his lackey left to prepare to capture the woman and kill the Angel.

8.

Thomas returned Grace to the room they had been allocated. He ushered her through the door and closed it behind him. She wriggled out of the chains and ran at him, her fingers clawed, nails scratching at him. She shrieked like a banshee as he grabbed her, picking her up easily.

"You asshole! You miserable bastard!" Tears streamed over her cheeks as he carried her struggling body to the bed.

Thomas threw her down on the soft mattress where she continued to scream insults at him. His hand covered her mouth, her curses muffled as she continued her tirade against him.

"Grace, be quiet." Thomas spoke softly.

She bit down hard on his hand, he winced but kept it positioned over her mouth.

"Will you please listen to me? Everything I said in there about keeping you as my slave was a lie."

Grace stopped struggling and became silent. Her eyes searched his for the truth. She mumbled and Thomas took his hand from her mouth. "What about the story of your falling? Was that a lie too?"

"Sadly, that part was true. I told you I had done something bad. I was blinded by wrath, rage, hatred, lust, horrible emotions which drove me to my fall." Thomas lowered his head, his wings slumped with his shoulders. "Repentance is not enough to redeem myself, I must be forgiven for my sins with love." He sighed. "Or at least that is what a battle Demon friend once told me."

"Was that… what's his name…? Dominus?"

"Decimus." Thomas corrected her. "Yes, just before we learned his lover, Eve had been captured by his enemy in order to try to bring him back into the Demon army. He told me perhaps love would be the great redeemer." He smiled at her, something shining in his eyes. "I'd like to think it's true." He caressed her face.

Grace shifted on the bed, moving toward him. She took his face in her hands and drew his lips to hers. She kissed him gently, lovingly, her tongue slipping across his lips, begging him to open to her. When he did, she deepened her kiss, tasting his tongue, the soft tissues of his mouth. She moaned softly as his hands moved across the tops of her breasts, caressing gently, lovingly. Her heart filled with warmth as he found his place in her arms. In truth, her heart was already chained to him.

He lay her down on the bed and removed the corset dress she had worn to the dinner. Her breasts perfect in the candlelight. Thomas' mouth moved softly over the sweet peaks of her nipples, tasting, licking, and suckling the soft woman beneath his lips.

Grace moaned and writhed beneath him, her body responsive to the touch of an Angel. The warm wetness spread from the curls of her mons. She was hot, wet and ready for him.

Thomas removed his clothing, standing in the flickering glow of the candles. His body sculpted by muscle and revealed in sharp planes of shadow and light to entice her. His erect cock stood proudly to attention as he raked his eyes over her body.

"Grace…" He climbed onto the bed. Moving over her, he felt her heat on his skin.

She shivered softly beneath him, not from cold but from sweet anticipation. Her hands reached up to his shoulders as he straddled her. His cock pressed against her belly. Thomas leaned on his elbows and removed the collar and chain from around her neck, dropping them both to the floor beside the bed with a clatter.

His hands traced down her temples, and along her jawline, his lips following contours he was becoming familiar with. Each time he explored her, he discovered a new place to make her moan, and writhe beneath him at the pleasurable sensations he brought. He felt his cock jerk slightly as she touched the hard planes of his chest, her nimble fingers running down to his abdominals, tracing the muscular structure. Her breath caught when he leaned forward and captured her lips with his own. Thomas eased himself between her spread thighs.

The head of his cock touched the damp folds between her legs. He smiled, knowing how ready she was for him. He took hold of his erection and gently rubbed the head between the slit in languorous motions, pressing harder when he reached her clit, making her moan his name softly between her parted lips. He slowly pressed himself between her slick folds, breaching her inner womanhood slowly. She arched against him, urging him to take her deeper. He complied, finally filling her. Thomas kissed her neck softly as he began to thrust inside her. Grace raked her nails down his back, her legs twining around his, trying to bring him deeper still within her already-full pussy.

Her soft moans and gasps were music to his ears as he loved her, her body a temple to be worshiped ardently by him, and him alone. He knew there was no other for him. Even Eve, whom he had fallen for back when he had first met her and Decimus, was no longer close to his heart as Grace was. Beneath him, Grace urged him to greater heights of passion. She reached down and slipped a hand between their thrusting bodies. Fingers slipped around his shaft as he drove inside her. Her thumb finding her clit and gently circling it. She moaned against him, her body tightening around his cock. Thomas groaned as the sensations drove him closer to his own primal need for release.

He gasped as she clenched around him, her body trembling with the sweet release of orgasm. Her pussy wet and dripping as she shuddered beneath him, he following suit a moment later, groaning out his climax as he came within her. He rested a moment, poised above her, but still joined. His breathing shadowing hers in hard, rough gasps of completion. Thomas withdrew slowly and sat back on his haunches, watching as his seed slowly dripped from her.

"That is a beautiful sight." His voice was breathless.

Grace flushed with embarrassment and tried to bring her knees together to hide herself from his heated gaze.

Thomas grabbed her knees and pushed them gently apart. "Never be ashamed of your beauty, Grace, never with me." He leaned down and pressed a kiss to her moist lips, before he moved up between her parted thighs and pressed his wet lips against hers, offering her a taste of their sex. Grace licked his lips clean before he deepened the kiss.

Thomas reluctantly pulled away and moved to the side, helping her to slip beneath the covers before he too followed her between the sheets. "We need to rest tonight, tomorrow we have a journey to make, and a sister to rescue."

Grace snuggled beside him. "What if we're too late? What if we can't get her out?"

"We will find a way, sweetheart." Thomas kissed the top of her head.

"We will find a way."

The sun shone on the road ahead, they left the slave trading post behind. Both were more than grateful they had left the wretched place. Other travelers were heading toward the town, some with slaves, tied or collared and in states of disbelief, misery or sad acceptance. There were people pushing carts or old trailers with goods. The occasional vehicle passed them, thick black smoke choking the pedestrians as they moved out of the way.

Grace removed her collar and chain as soon as they were out of the view of the town. Her neck was chafed from the rough leather collar made for a dog with fur to protect its skin.

Thomas softly kissed the red, raw spots on her neck, her breaths came in soft, sweet pants. He pulled away, smiling.

"My sweetheart, we can't do it here, we need to get moving. Maximus' city is still a few days travel at least." He gathered her hand and kissed the knuckles. "But, tonight, if you are not too tired, and we can find a safe place to rest, then…" He allowed his unspoken words to hang in the air, let his promise of untold delights arouse her.

It was nearing sunset when they heard the faint sound of a motorcycle approaching them. Thomas moved to the side, of the road, gently pulling Grace along with him. She was slow to move; footsore and exhaustion from the long day's walk making her sluggish. She felt him tug on her hand and realized he had moved away from her, their arms stretched out between them. The roar of the motorcycle became louder.

Grace turned to face the sunset and placed her hand up to shade her eyes from the glare. She was momentarily blinded by the light of the setting sun. Thomas called to her again over the roar of the engine as the motorcycle drew closer.

A sidecar was attached to the motorcycle. A man leaned from it as he passed and grabbed Grace, pulling her free of Thomas' grip. She screamed, struggling against the side of the sidecar as the man pulled her in.

Thomas roared and started after them. He took a few running steps and sprang into the air. His wings spread wide with an audible snap of feathers. He gave chase to Grace's kidnappers, he could hear her screams over the roar of the motorcycle. She struggled in the arms of her captors. His wings beat furiously as he gained on them.

The sun sparkled off something metallic held by the pillion passenger and caught his eye. A gun was aimed toward Thomas. He darted away and the first shot whizzed by his ear. His heart hammered in his chest, fear coursed through his system. Adrenalin and anger spurred him on. Another shot rang out as he gained ground on the kidnappers. He could hear the men shouting at each other. The man in the sidecar telling the driver to keep the bike steady. Grace struggled against her captor. Her screams for him reached deep into his heart.

He flapped his wings harder, trying to gain what distance he had lost by dodging the bullets. He was almost above them and ready to dive when another shot rang out.

Feathers flew and searing pain lanced through his left wing. Grace's screams were blood curdling when she saw the blood covering his wing. He lost altitude and control, veering off and crashing heavily into a group of trees on the side of the road. The motorcycle's rumbling gradually faded as he fell to the ground, exhausted and in agony. He breathed deeply and placed a hand over his damaged wing. Thomas hissed in pain as the fire of the wound burst through his body, causing stars to flare up before his eyes. His hand came back bloodied, small pieces of broken feathers attached. He groaned as he struggled to his feet.

Small pieces of sticks and twigs pierced him. Wincing, he pulled the offending pieces from his body. He tested his injured wing. It had already stiffened up with his blood drying quickly against the feathers. The sound of the motorcycle rushed back and passed him at a high speed, they were headed back to where he had come from.

Grace's screams hovered on the wind as they sped past him. He sprinted back to the road, breaking from the cover of the trees and scrub where he had crash landed. The motorcycle roared off into the distance, his heart broke as Grace disappeared from his sight. Determination to get her back burned deep within his heart. He knew where they were taking her.

Tobias would pay.

9.

Grace's face throbbed where she had been struck. She slowly opened her eyes to find herself spread eagled on a satin-covered four poster bed. She tried to move, her hands and feet met the cutting resistance of ropes tied securely, binding her tightly. Her neck felt tight, she looked down to see a chain leading from her neck to a metal ring secured to the head of the bed. She sighed softly, a sob escaping her lips.

Movement in the shadows caught her eye. "Ah, I see my guest is awake." The unmistakable voice of Tobias caught her full attention.

"Why am I here? Why have you taken me? Where is Thomas?" Her voice hitched with sobs, belying her fear.

Tobias leaned forward into a patch of light from the open fire burning in a hearth beside him. His angled features casting shadows across half his face, and his wings behind him made him appear like a herald of doom. The smile on his face confirmed her fears.

"You are here because I want you to be here. You have been taken because you killed one of my men, and his brother wants payback." He stood and approached the bed. Grace wriggled away from him, her heart rate rising a few notches. He leaned down and gently caressed her face. She shuddered at his touch, and his next words chilled her. "And your beloved Thomas," his lips pressed against her ear as he whispered. "Is dead. Shot from the sky."

He stood upright as she began to sob, her body shaking with the despair from his statement.

"No," she whispered. "He can't be."

"He is, and tonight, you will be my bedmate. I may keep you for a night, or a week before I give you over to your new owner." Tobias took Grace's chin in his hand and leaned down. He pressed his lips against hers, his tongue swiping across the swollen lips of her mouth. Grace pulled away, wincing as his grip tightened on her chin. "But, if you please me, I may keep you all to myself."

Tobias grinned. "Until tonight, my treasure." He turned and walked to the door. "Oh and by the way… your sister? The one you are looking for, Ebony?" He stopped with his hand on the doorknob. "She made it to Maximus' city. Apparently, he had some fun with her, before she escaped. The word is, she was picked up by some raiders to the west. More than likely, she's being gangbanged by them right this minute." Tobias smiled cruelly. "You are much better off here, rather than out there." He left her alone, her heart broken.

Thomas moved slowly, painfully. His determination forced him to run until he almost collapsed with exhaustion. He had to get her back. The blood flow had stopped from the wound on his wing. Fortunately it was a clean wound, the bullet having gone through the thin flesh of his wing. The force of the impact knocking him about and down into the trees had caused him more aches and pains than he cared to have. The road stretched out before him, the single dot in the distance showing him his destination.

He flexed his wings, trying to get the left one working again. The pain shot through his body but the wing moved. Much of the damage had healed and the injury had closed over, thanks to the rapid healing of Angel physiology. He could handle this. He took a tentative step and leapt into the air. His wings held him up as he flapped. He sighed in relief, but winced at the pain. He drew his sword and checked the sharpness. He swung it experimentally, the blade whistling in the air, its voice singing through the air along with his wings.

It was time to go and get his love back from the clutches of an Angel who had turned very bad.

Grace trembled on the bed, her body stripped of her clothing, her hands and feet bound to the four posts of the bed with strong leather ties which had replaced the ropes binding her. Tobias entered the room. Her fear was palpable in the air as her eyes followed him. The erection he sported tented the robe he wore. Her captor crossed to a buffet where a selection of spirits waited in bottles and decanters. He poured himself a glass of whiskey and downed it before turning to her. The drinking glass clinking against the polished glass top of the buffet

An ornate glass roof allowed the brilliant light of the moon to shine down over the area before the bed. Tobias walked slowly into the light, his steps predatory, as if he was approaching a sacrifice on an altar. He smiled darkly as he climbed on top of the bed, his body covering hers.

His lips touched her flesh, her stomach churned as she struggled against her bonds. Tobias sat back, straddling her. He pulled the robe from his body, revealing his muscular chest and arms. His hard cock strained upward to his abdomen. Grace closed her eyes, the tears trailing down her temples at the hopelessness of her situation. She felt him move closer to her. Hot breath preceded his tongue lapping at her salty tears, she turned her head to the side, trying to escape his attentions. She opened her eyes as he shifted away, rearing up above her like a conquering villain.

A shadow on the floor behind the bed distracted her a moment before the glass roof shattered behind them and a large figure dropped to the glass covered ground.

Tobias turned sharply at the shattering sounds. he rose, his fists curled to strike at the intruder.

Thomas.

Thomas moved in a blur of fury, striking Tobias with his fists, pummelling the Fallen to the ground where he lay bruised and battered. A fast motion and a sickening wet sound greeted her ears as Thomas unsheathed and lifted his sword above Tobias and brought it down.

Tobias screamed as one of his wings was sliced from his body. Blood spurted out, covering the clean white bone and Tobias' naked back as Thomas swiftly changed the angle of his stroke and cleaved the other wing from Tobias' body. The Fallen tipped forward and fell to the floor with an agonised cry. He writhed on the floor, his screams sharp in the room as his blood pumped from the wounds where his wings once were.

Thomas sliced through the bonds holding Grace's feet tied to the posts. He moved swiftly to cut through the other bonds. She rose to meet her lover, her arms wrapping tightly around him as she sobbed

"He told me you were dead," she whispered softly, as he held her against his chest.

Thomas held her in his arms tightly, never wanting to let her go. He pulled away from her to check over her body. "Are you all right? Did he…?" His face showed his concern.

"No, he didn't take me." Her smile was weak, watery but joyful. Thomas heard a groan from the end of the bed, pushed away from Grace and took up his sword.

"For your sins, I, Thomas, condemn you, Tobias the Fallen, to death." Tobias got to his knees weakly and looked up as Thomas lifted the blade and swung. The head of the Fallen Angel rolled across the carpet, blood spurted from the open hole of his neck as his heart pumped its final beat. Grace watched wide-eyed as the headless corpse slumped to the floor.

Thomas wiped the blade on the satin bedcover before holding his hand out to Grace. "Come, sweetheart, let's get you out of here."

Grace scrambled off the bed and into his arms, Thomas helped her to a wardrobe where they found suitable clothing for her to wear. She dressed quickly, explaining to Thomas everything that Tobias had told her about her sister.

When she had dressed, Thomas glanced up at the smashed window. Large shards of glass made their escape impossible. "Come." Thomas gathered her hand in his. "We will have to get out through the building, there's got to be a way out of here. Once we get outside, I'll fly us out and we can continue to look for Ebony."

Grace looked up at Thomas, her eyes filled with worry. He leaned down and kissed her tenderly. "Let's go." He opened the door up and peeked out. There were two Demon guards standing at the end of the corridor.

"Stay here while I handle this." Thomas turned to her. "Should anything happen to me, I want you to run, get out of here as fast as you can. Don't stop for anything." He gazed deeply into her eyes and kissed her with a fierce passion.

"Don't go getting yourself killed on me, I couldn't bear losing you again." Grace clutched hard against the warmth of his chest, ignoring the stickiness of Tobias' blood.

"I have no intentions of losing my life today." Thomas pressed his lips to her hair. "Just stay here, I'll be back for you." He turned and stalked toward his prey, movingh silently with sword in hand.

The guards were quietly chatting to each other about the human whores and which ones they preferred. A quick flash of Thomas's bloodied blade and the pair crumpled to the floor. Their heads left their shoulders, one after the other, with silent screams. Grace watched from the doorway of Tobias' quarters, biting her lower lip as she watched the carnage wrought by her Angel lover.

He was a magnificent warrior, his body framed by his beautiful wings, the smattering of black feathers sharp against the purity of the white. Grace's heart beat hard in her chest as she watched him creep back to her. His breathing steady. His hand out in invitation for her to join him. She slipped her small hand into his large one.

A jolt of *something* raced through her hand and into her body. It tore through her system, straight to her core. Her eyes locked onto his and she smiled. Grace leaned down and picked up one of the fallen guard's weapons, a small rifle, as they passed. She checked both bodies for more ammunition for her newly acquired prize, pocketing more rounds for the rifle before she held it ready.Grace wasn't an expert in using a gun, but she had gone paintballing many times with friends before the world went to shit, that and the duck shooting gallery at the yearly show had helped her to know something about firing a gun.

Grace followed Thomas down the corridor to what she hoped was the way out, and freedom.

"Almost there," Thomas said. They turned right and headed toward a small terrace. The glass door was locked. He didn't want to attract attention by smashing it so he hid Grace in a small alcove, behind a curtain while he went back to search for the keys to the door. He hoped to find a master key on the guards or at least on Tobias' corpse. He came back empty-handed. "I'll have to do this the old-fashioned way." He muttered, picked up a stone pedestal and lobbed it through the glass doors.

Grace flinched as the shattering glass echoed through the halls, causing shouts to echo back.

"Come on, time to leave." Thomas grabbed her hand and led her out onto the moonlit terrace. Thomas swept Grace into his arms and launched off the terrace into the night. His wings beating hard against the chill air as they ascended into the sky. Grace cuddled herself hard against Thomas' armour as the lands below them flew past.

"We need to head to the west, that's where Tobias told me my sister had been taken by the raiders." Thomas nodded and banked, heading toward the west.

10.

Thomas landed a few hours later, exhaustion overwhelming him as his feet touched the ground. There was an abandoned farmhouse nearby and Grace helped her fatigued lover to the battered front door.

The sun was starting to rise as she helped him to the dust covered mattress in the main bedroom. Grace covered him with a blanket after shaking it free of dust. "I'll see what I can scrounge up to eat, if there's anything in the cupboards." She left him to doze.

She located the kitchen, lay down her gun and opened several cupboards, searching for anything edible. There was nothing in the kitchen, and a near-barren vegetable patch was all that remained of the farm's home garden. Grace turned around and was faced with the double barrels of a shotgun, wielded by a masked man. A hand went around her mouth from behind, another secured her arms, holding her tight against a body-armoured chest.

"Don't move, don't scream." A rough voice whispered in her ear. "Where's the other one, the Angel who flew you here?" Her captor softened his grip on her mouth to let her respond

"What Angel? I came here alone."

"Don't bother, we know he's here. Where is he?" Grace's eyes flicked to the doorway leading to the bedroom.

"Good girl." A sack was pushed over her head, depriving her of sight. "This is going to sting, but I'm sorry, it's necessary.

"What?" Grace registered shock at the suggestion pain would be necessary. "Please, no, I'll come quietly, I'm not going to fight you." A damp swab, smelling of alcohol was swiped over her shoulder. She struggled, despite being held firm. Her captors cursed, and another set of hands gripped her shoulders, securing her.

She felt the sting and the rush of something cold as it entered her bloodstream. "No, please…" she whimpered as darkness swirled and she was drawn into a deeper, darker hole. The sounds, already muffled by her hood became dimmer, softer and confusing.

"He's awake. Hold him down, get the damned Taser." A pair of her captor's hands left her body, leaving behind the sensation of warmth..

Grace felt her legs weaken and numb as the sedative worked through her body. She was gently lowered to the ground as the sounds of a Taser being used reached her ears.

"That's got him…"

Thomas' head and body felt like he had taken the long, and painful trip down to Hell, hitting every jagged rock along the way. He opened his eyes to a stark white ceiling, and a fan spinning lazily above him. It didn't seem to be moving much air around at all, the room was hot and stuffy. He took a chance and glanced around, a young woman with dark hair sat on the only other piece of furniture in his room. A folding chair.

"You're awake." She said, showing him her fabulous powers of observation.

"Yes, I am. Where's Grace?"

"Who are you to her?" The woman's voice was sharp, something about her eyes was familiar.

"I'm a friend." Thomas was wary.

"Really?" His interrogator stood and moved closer to his bed.

"What about this?" She pulled a collar and leash from a bag and threw it against his naked chest.

Thomas noted he was bare, naked as the day he was made, only a thin sheet covered his abdomen. He also noticed the young woman didn't seem to care, she was far too angry.

"What about it?"

"Are you a slaver? Do you own her?" The woman's voice spat like a hissing cat. "Or are you into some kind of sick kink? I know she isn't into that sort of thing."

"How?" Thomas asked, trying to sit up but finding his arms bound to the bed. "How do you know she's not into the whole Master and slave thing?" He looked closely at her. Why did she look so familiar?

"Because, she's my sister." She glared at Thomas. The door opened and a Demon entered. He glanced from the dark-haired woman, he and Grace had been searching for and smiled, his eyes softening with an emotion that Thomas rarely saw in a Demon. Love.

"Ebony, you are not supposed to be in here with him, not until we can ascertain his motives." The Demon set aside the tray he held in his hands to focus on the woman.

"Auxilio." Ebony turned toward him, "He's bound and may have more information on Grace, she has barely spoken. She's been badly hurt and I want to know why."

"You have not seen her yet. You have only second-hand information on which to make that assumption. She is still sleeping." The Demon stepped forward and gently caressed Ebony's cheek. With care, and deliberate slowness, as if he were reluctant to take his touch from her face, he tucked an errant strand of hair behind her ear. Thomas watched the exchange with guarded interest.

"Go and see her, calm your fears and be at peace. Rejoice in your reunion." His voice was soothing. "She will be overjoyed to see you when she awakens."

Ebony nodded, throwing Thomas a rueful look before she walked past Auxilio and closed the door.

"Forgive my Ebony, she can be something of a fire-demon when she gets worked up." He gave Thomas a friendly smile.

Thomas regarded the Demon before him, kept his mouth shut, and his thoughts to himself.

"I'm sorry we had to knock both you and Grace out in order to bring you here. Our position is quite precarious, and we are often under the scrutiny of hunting parties." Auxilio retrieved the tray and set it down beside Thomas's bed.

"So, we have ascertained that the young woman whom we brought in with you is my Ebony's sister, Grace. A woman we have been seeking for over a month, but that begs the question… who are you?" Auxilio picked up a clean white cloth and dipped it into water, clouded with antiseptic.

Thomas watched as the Demon squeezed the water from the cloth and gently applied it to the slowly healing wound in his wing, as well as the damage to his flesh by the tree branches and the glass through which he had crashed to save Grace from Tobias.

"I am Thomas, an Angel of Mercy." He winced as the pain of the antiseptic shot through the damaged skin

"An almost *Fallen* Angel of Mercy." Auxilio observed. "Tell me, how many more feathers must you lose to blackness before you fall completely?" Auxilio leaned his arm on his knee and studied Thomas.

"Not many."

Auxilio smiled ruefully. "I suspected as much." He picked up a bandage and held it, his eyes taking in the state of the Angel before him. "Now if I release you, will you allow me to bind your injuries? I mean you no harm. However, if Ebony discovers you have injured or molested her sister in any way, I cannot guarantee *she* won't try to tear your head off." He smiled. "She is quite a passionate woman."

"I can see that." Thomas nodded his agreement. "I swear to you, I will not cause harm to you, or any under your protection for so long as I am in your presence, and within the safety of your home.”

“Good enough.” Auxilio nodded and unbound Thomas.

The Angel sat up slowly, Auxilio helping him with a supportive hand on his back. “So tell me, how did you come across Grace?”

While the Demon wrapped the linen around his injuries, Thomas recounted his meeting Grace. Their time as Tobias’ guest, capture by his men and their subsequent escape. All culminating with their capture by Auxilio’s men. One wing would be bound and useless while the bullet wound healed, and the numerous scrapes and gashes on his body would cause him to feel stiff and sore for a few days.

“Well, now you’re up and about, allow me to show you around my ‘home’ such as it is, and tell you something about what we do down here.” Auxilio stood and removed the tray from the floor.

11.

"Gracie, wake up." Ebony's voice drifted through the dream. Grace wept, her hands reaching out to Ebony as she felt her body being pulled away.

"Ebony." Grace's voice slurred as the haze of the sedative wore off. The world was dim around her when she opened her eyes. The sounds dull in her ears became stronger, less muted. The foul taste in her mouth hit her full force, churning her empty stomach

Grace sat up, her movements sluggish. Ebony supported her while holding a bottle of water to her sister's lips. "Drink, it will help diminish the effects of the sedative.

Grace drank greedily. Water trickled down her chin as she guzzled the clear, refreshing liquid. Once she had regained enough focus, Grace studied her sister. "Ebony, is it really you?" Grace caressed her sister, her fingers checking for injuries. Overwhelmed, the sister she thought had been lost, was safe.

"Yeah, it's me, sis. I'm okay. I'm alive." Ebony smiled softly at her sister.

Grace reached out and pulled her into a tight hug. Tears cascaded over her cheeks. "I thought I'd lost you. I was coming to find you, tracking as best I could. But I got ambushed, an Angel saved me." Grace eased away. Tears ran freely. "His name is Thomas, do you know where he is?" She sat forward and moaned as her head spun with the aftereffects of the sedative.

"He's with us. He's fine, Auxilio is taking care of him." Ebony moved to a footlocker and withdrew some clothes. "Here, put these on and we'll go and get you some food." Ebony handed the clothing to her sister.

"Who is Auxilio?" Grace slipped on the tee-shirt over her bra and struggled into a pair of jeans.

Her sister smiled; a soft dreamy smile. "Auxilio is a Battle Demon. He leads the rebellion against Maximus. When I was kidnapped, I was taken to Maximus, after a short stop in the trading post nearby. Auxilio was one of his men who arrived to take us into the city from the Slavers. Maximus took me as one of his harem." Ebony paused to open the door, once Grace had finished dressing.

"Auxilio helped me, and several other slaves, to escape. A short time later, we became lovers." Ebony turned to face her sister, expecting ridicule, or berating, over her choice of lover.

Instead, Grace smiled and pulled Ebony into a tight embrace. "I'm grateful to him for saving you." She kissed her sister's cheek.

"I'm glad you're safe." They continued down the corridor and into the main area. They were in a section of underground tunnels. Train tracks ran through the center, a dim glow and the noise of people talking softly echoed down the smoothed tunnel walls.

"Where are we?" Grace asked.

"The underground Metro system, at a station at the end of the line. It's as far as we can get out of the city without actually leaving it. From here, we co-ordinate raiding groups to free slaves being brought into the city, and some a bit further afield, like on the major highways leading in. It's a constant battle between us, the Slavers and Maximus. Auxilio wants to take Maximus down and end his evil reign in the city."

Grace scanned the area as they approached the main area of the underground train station. Men and women moved around, attending to chores. Two youths were sorting through tin cans, and packets of dried foods, organizing them into piles before packing them into clear plastic tubs

"The scavenging teams have arrived back. They go through the abandoned parts of the city, through deserted houses and shops trying of find food and other useful supplies, like we used to do." Ebony nodded to the two youths as they walked past. "The section where we had you, we use as a holding area for prisoners, Thomas was in a room nearby. You weren't there because I didn't trust you, it's just Auxilio doesn't trust anyone he doesn't know. When we discovered you were traveling with an Angel, I had to calm him down, before you could be brought in."

Grace nodded. "It's okay, I understand. I probably would have done the same thing." Grace draped her arm around Ebony's shoulders.

"Come on, let's go get something to eat." Ebony walked her past the youths, and their sorting, to a small area which housed a café. It had been used when people took the train to work of a morning.

They sat down after collecting a small serving of instant noodles and a tin of peach halves. The savory scent of the noodles and their flavoring set Grace's stomach rumbling.

"Sorry it's not fresh food. We're working on getting a hydroponics set up in place." Ebony twirled some noodles around her fork.

"We make do with what we have; there are many more out there with less, or nothing." An unfamiliar voice chided gently.

Ebony's face lit up as she turned to face the large, muscular Demon behind her.

"Auxilio." She sprang to her feet and wrapped her arms around the huge man. "This is my sister, Grace." Ebony introduced her sister to her lover. "Grace - Auxilio."

Grace stood but not longer saw Auxilio. Behind him stood Thomas, looking a little worse for wear but much better than when she had left him to rest in the bed of the abandoned house. He smiled and held his arms open for her.

"Thomas," Grace whispered, hot tears trickled down her cheeks as she ran to him. He stumbled a little as she impacted against the scarred and muscled body of her Angel lover.

"I'm all right, Grace, I was more worried for you." He soothed her, stroking her back. "Your sister subjected me to quite a threatening interrogation when I awoke."

Grace glanced at Ebony, who had the decency to look ashamed. "I'm sorry but I had to know what your motives, and intentions, toward my sister were."

"Well, now we are all here and together, I think it's time we spoke about a few things which may be important to our girls.

After they have eaten, of course." Auxilio nodded to the table with their unfinished meals.

Grace extricated herself from Thomas' arms and quickly finished her meal, beside Ebony. Thomas watched the two sisters, love in his heart for his Grace, and admiration for her sister. Auxilio had told him of their escape from Maximus, Ebony had had a rough time. Though she seemed to be healing emotionally now, he knew the scars of her enslavement would remain within her mind for many years to come.

12.

Grace and Ebony settled onto a worn-looking couch while Thomas and Auxilio leaned against a desk in the stationmaster's office.

Auxilio sighed and rubbed the back of his neck in consternation. "It's not easy for me to tell you this, but you were both targets for Maximus' harem."

"What do you mean, targets?" Ebony questioned.

"Tell me what you recall of the night your community was attacked?" Auxilio asked the girls.

Ebony seemed pensive, as though the night was still too fresh in her mind. "I remember being woken in the middle of the night. Someone was shouting, raiders had broken through the gate. We grabbed what little we could and ran. By then, the town was overwhelmed and we barely made our escape. There were only a handful of others who also escaped."

"The raid was set up by one of your residents. Someone who had earned the town's trust. Do you know a man named Ryan Bertrell?"

Ebony nodded. "I remember him, he was one of the men who worked as a guard in town. He was always trying to get me to sleep with him. I didn't like him; he creeped me out." She shuddered at the memory of the horrible man.

"I agree. He was a horrible sleaze," Grace admitted.

"It was him who made a deal with Maximus to take you." Auxilio crossed his arms and peered at the ground. "He came to the city one day posing as a trader. He gained an audience with Maximus and told him of how beautiful you both are. He made a deal with Maximus, the Demon could have Grace if Bertrell was allowed to take you as his slave. Maximus is a greedy Demon, and he wasn't content to only take Grace. He double crossed Ryan."

"How do you know this?" Ebony gazed at Auxilio.

"I was the one who volunteered to pick you both up at the trading post. I wanted to see the two women Maximus was going to destroy."

"What? Why?" Fear and anger rose in Grace as she stood and stepped toward Thomas.

Behind her Ebony sobbed quietly. "Why didn't you tell me?" Her lover moved toward her and crouched at her feet.

Thomas pulled Grace into his arms. Her body trembld in anger and he tried to soothe her.

"I didn't want you to think less of me, I was afraid you would run from me. The minute I saw you, I knew you were not for Maximus. You didn't deserve his touch; the damage he would have, *has,* done to you." He gathered her hands in his and dusted her knuckles with kisses. "I don't know if I could have helped you to heal once he tired of you and tossed you aside. It would have been like the other girls I couldn't save." Auxilio gazed into Ebony's tear-filled eyes. He gently wiped at the falling droplets, catching them before they fell from her chin. "Sweetheart, I could not let him hurt you again. I will not let him do this to another. We have had word of another group of slavers bringing in a fresh run of slaves, recent captures. Maximus will be inspecting them when they arrive in a few days." He stood, releasing her hands and turned to Thomas.

"We need your help, Thomas."

Thomas kept his arms around Grace where she felt safe and secure. "What do you need me to do?"

"I need you to deliver us all to Maximus."

Ebony's response was sharp. She stood and slapped Auxilio hard across the face. "Are you insane? He'll kill you, and… and…, you know how I suffered at his hands. Yet you want to deliver me, and my sister into his waiting arms?" She paced back and forth, her fingertips turning blue with the ferocity of her twisting her hands in each other. "Why? Why would you do this?"

"Maximus knows me, but Thomas is an unknown. I can sneak weapons into the city and talk to the many other Demons and men who would be interested in getting vengeance against Maximus. He deserves to die."

Ebony stopped in front of him. "Yes, but you don't deserve to die." She pushed past him, angry tears dripping as she stormed away.

Grace pulled away from Thomas to go after her.

"Leave her be, Grace." Auxilio placed a hand on her shoulder to prevent her from following her sister. "When I rescued your sister she was in a terrible state. Maximus, he… he had hurt her. Badly." Shame burned his face. "I didn't have the chance to stop him, or get her out of the city in time."

"He raped her?" Grace turned from the door Ebony had slammed through to face the Demon who had his hand on her shoulder. Tobias' last words screamed at her - "*Maximus had some fun with her before she escaped.*

The pain in Auxilio's eyes confirmed what she had suspected and voiced. "I'm afraid so. When I found her, she was broken. I was terrified for her. I had to force feed her for a week. She refused to speak, wouldn't move from her bed until I told her of my growing feelings for her. I convinced her, she was stronger than Maximus and would survive him. I swore to her that he would die at my hand. She agreed to allow me to help her, as long as she could watch the light dying from his eyes as I killed him." He walked back to the desk and flopped down in the desk chair. "Those were her first words she spoke to me after I rescued her. *As long as I can watch the light die from his eyes and hear him take his last breath.* Those were her exact words."

"You're going to put us all in danger because she wants to see the man who tormented her, die?" Grace had trouble wrapping her head around the situation.

"Maximus is not a man, he is a Demon. He is capable of inflicting unimaginable hurt. I have turned away from the darkness to seek my own redemption, such as it might be. Thomas has the darkness on his wings, I can only imagine what he has done to earn the path to the Fall." Auxilio nodded to Thomas.

"There are certain things he has told me, I know of his sins. I forgive him for those transgressions, and any in the future which he has no control over. But ,to place Ebony and myself in danger?" Grace shook her head in defiance. "It's not acceptable. We've lost so much and only just found each other again."

"Grace." Thomas gathered her into his strong arms. "If we do nothing, many more lives will be shattered by Demons like Maximus. Remember I told you of Marius who took my friend Decimus' beloved? He too was a creature of pure darkness. A Demon whose every pore on his body exuded evil. They are two of the same."

"Maximus is perhaps even worse. Thomas, do you know of any others who might be willing to come and aid us?" Auxilio asked.

"I might, but to go to them is a journey which will take more than two days in flight."

"And you are not at your full strength." Auxilio thought for a moment. "Perhaps we can change our plans a little. Maximus has placed a bounty on my head, Ebony and Grace's. I can arrange for the incoming slaves to be intercepted before they reach the city, they can help us. It will be tricky, but we need as many warriors on our side as possible. I'm sure they would rather fight than become slaves to Maximus. Grace would you go and find Ebony, check if she's alright?" Auxilio asked her.

She seemed hesitant to leave. Thomas looked down at her, caressing her face. "Go, everything will be fine, I promise." Grace nodded and left reluctantly.

She left the office and walked down through the station. Angels, Demons and men were scattered about, while women and children sorted out more food and clothing. They all wore the weary look of refugees, displaced and afraid for the future. But, behind the despair, there was a light of hope shining in the darkness. She hoped Auxilio's plan worked. For all their sakes.

13.

Thomas flew through the night, his wings aching but determination fuelling his flight. Grace had sobbed hard against his chest, her arms clutching his torso as she begged him to stay safe. He knew there was a chance he might not make it back, but he was well rested after waiting with the women and those who could not make it to the raid to rescue the slaves initially intended for Maximus' city.

Before long, the devastated lands below turned into arable farmland more familiar to Thomas. He soared toward Eve and Decimus' farm. He landed at dawn's first blush in the east to be faced with the tips of swords pointed at his throat.

"It's Thomas." Octavius spoke with relief. "Hail, friend." The Demon smiled, lowered his weapon and sheathed it. Thomas nodded, breathless after his exhausting flight.

The powerful figure of Decimus strode toward him from the nearby farmhouse. The dawn sunlight shone on his black wings, the crimson sheen illuminated against the sunlight.

"Thomas!" Decimus cried joyously. "Welcome home."

Behind him, a squeal of joy was followed by Eve's appearance. She ran and threw her arms around the Angel. "Thomas, we wondered when we'd get you back!" She kissed his cheek. "Are you back for a while?"

"No, no my friend." Thomas hugged her tight. "I have come to ask Decimus and our brothers for a favor." Thomas peered at Decimus.

"What do you need, my friend?" Decimus asked.

"Can we go into the house; I need something to eat and drink. I have much to tell you."

Decimus draped an arm around Thomas and helped the tired Angel into the farmhouse; Eve opened the door for them. The other Demons returned to their work, patrolling the farmhouse grounds or returning to the fields to work the crops.

Thomas sat down at the small kitchen table while Eve headed for the kitchen to prepare something to eat. She returned with a glass of cool water, which he downed quickly and she refilled it for him from a pitcher.

Decimus and Octavius joined him at the table, anxious to hear what Thomas had to say. The delicious aroma of cooking assailed his senses as he began to explain. He told of his travels, his meeting of Grace and their discovery her sister, Ebony was the lover of a Demon and helping to free captured slaves.

Eve's coughing fit from the kitchen had Decimus up and at her side in a flash as she retched and vomited into the kitchen sink. Thomas watched, worriedly as Decimus soothed her.

"Fine, I'll be fine." She wiped her mouth, rinsed the sink and washed her hands before she handed the cooking duties over to Decimus. She left the kitchen to clean herself up properly.

Decimus brought a plate of food over to Thomas.

"Is she all right?" Thomas asked as Decimus sat opposite him.

The battle Demon smiled. "She'll be fine. It's morning sickness; she's pregnant."

"*Pregnant?* How is that even possible?" Thomas sounded incredulous.

"Well, when a Demon and a human love each other very much, they go to bed. But, we don't get very much sleep and…" Thomas threw a pea at Decimus while Octavius attempted to stifle his laughter.

"I know the mechanics. I wasn't sure it was possible, between humans and Angels or Demons. I thought He took the ability to procreate away." Thomas was careful not to mention the Almighty by title or name in deference to the Demons in the room.

"Remember, He made us all in his own image. The same applies to humans. We were exalted as his first, so of course we are able to breed with them. I just wasn't expecting it to happen so soon." Decimus grinned, proud of his prowess.

"Oh really? So soon, you say." Eve stepped into the room and confronted her lover. "With the constant sex we've been having, *unprotected* sex I might add, it's no surprise you knocked me up."

Decimus had the grace to blush at Eve's words. "And I love that you are." He stood and swept her into his arms.

"Barefoot and pregnant?"

"Mine." Decimus smiled.

Thomas stood to embrace Eve and shake Decimus' hand. "It's great to hear you two are expecting. Congratulations to both of you."

Decimus sat."Now, we've got our happy news out of the way, let's get started on what you and Auxilio have planned. I think I recall him, though he was from another battle group than I was."

"Yes, he was of Maximus' Legion, second in command. He turned on him when he fell in love with Grace's sister. They escaped with a small group of slaves and Demons, and began to rescue other slaves." Thomas picked up the fork and continued to eat.

"What can we do to help?" Decimus asked.

"We need more warriors. Demons, Angels, even humans. Anyone who wants to come and help us to stop Maximus's reign. There are innocent people being hurt."

"It's happening a lot around the world today, too many Demons are gaining control. We have a few more Demons and a couple of Angels who have settled on the farm since you left us, Space is becoming a problem. If you can successfully remove Maximus from power, what are the chances that Auxilio will take his place? Will he rule for peace and harmony instead of self-interest?" Decimus stood and assisted Eve to sit.

"He seems honest, and loyal to those he loves. He showed me much of what he has accomplished in a short few weeks. He is a natural leader, and I think he might be able to take control of the city and use his power for peace, rather than his own agenda."

Decimus nodded at Thomas' assessment. "Very well, we'll leave for Auxilio's in the morning. Until then, rest and I'll inform the others. Any who wish to come will be made welcome." Decimus placed his hands gently on Eve's shoulders and rubbed them.

"Are you sure about this, Thomas?" she asked him.

"Yes, Eve. I'm certain."

Eve reached across and put her hand over his. "Please, make sure he comes home to me, to us." She placed a hand over her belly.

"I will," Thomas promised and in his heart, he hoped it was a promise he could keep.

14.

The fluttering of wings broke the stillness, and quiet, of the early morning as a large group of Demons and Angels took flight from the small farm. Two Demons and an Angel remained behind to protect the farm and the woman who had helped to give them a home. Tears had dampened Eve's cheeks when she'd kissed her lover goodbye. She watched and waved as he took to the skies. All had donned armor prior to ascending into the sky; it shone in the eerie dawn light.

It would take two days for them to arrive at their destination, exhausted and ready to take down another Demon who aspired to be a tyrant king.

Grace strolled through the quiet corridor, heading towards the Station Master's office. The door was unlocked, and the lighting was dim. She pushed open the door slowly, stopping when she heard the soft moans and whimpers of passion in the office.

Silhouetted against the dim light, Grace watched silently as Ebony rode Auxilio as he sat in the desk chair. His wings quivered in passion as his human lover rose and fell upon him in passion. Grace smiled, knowing her sister had found love and joy in the arms of a Demon, who obviously felt the same for her. She closed the door quietly, and headed back down to the concourse to help the scavenging teams sort their haul from the day's mission.

Ebony and Auxilio emerged a short time later. Auxilio headed toward the entrance. Grace had a 'just fucked' flush to her cheeks, and her hair was a little messy.

"Well, I'd ask what you two were up to, but I think I already know." Grace took a sip from a bottle of water and smirked.

"Oh shut up." Ebony pushed against her sister's shoulder. "When are we expecting Thomas and his friends back?"

"Today, hopefully. If he has managed to convince them to come, they would have left two days ago." Grace sighed. She missed Thomas desperately, and had found the last few days without him to be incredibly lonely. If not for her sister, she wasn't sure she would have survived with her sanity intact.

Auxilio returned to the concourse. Ebony's eyes locked on him as he strode towards the two women.

"There is a large group of Demons in flight, heading this way. We need to prepare for an attack." He moved swiftly to take both women by the arms and hauled them from their seats

"Could it be Thomas returning?" Grace hoped for the best.

"No, they are coming from the wrong direction. It's forces from Maximus' city who approach us.". He led the two women down a tunnel toward a section where other women and the children hid.

"You'll be safe here." Auxilio looked over the assembled women and children. "Stay here, don't come out until one of us comes down to get you. Perhaps they will pass us by, perhaps they will finally attack us, but you must be safe. Grace, Ebony knows of another tunnel we are certain Maximus doesn't know about. If need be, she will take you and the women and children out and away from here. We have a small area scouted out for a fall-back position, she will explain everything to you." Auxilio turned away, Ebony reached out and grabbed his arm.

"Be safe. I love you." She pulled him against her in a desperate embrace, their lips crushing against each other in a sweet, lingering kiss.

Reluctance to leave was clear in his eyes. Auxilio reached out and caressed Ebony's cheek. "I'll be back soon, don't worry."

Grace could have sworn, in his voice, there was the slightest tinge of doubt.

Auxilio watched as the dark cloud approached. He, and his brothers, wore their armor with pride. They knew there was much more at stake than their families. Their women and children hid below; their freedom was the prize to be won this day. He readied his sword and took to the skies, his brothers in arms following with a flutter of crimson-sheened wings.

Battle cries rang forth from the lips of their adversaries. Former brothers-in-arms clashed in the skies. Harsh scraping of metal-on-metal and the agonized screams of the wounded filled the air. Demonic swords struck exposed areas on bodies. Demons from both sides of the battle, dropped from the sky. Black feathers slicked with blood crashed to the earth followed by the dying and brutalized bodies of their owners. The sky overhead darkened as the battle continued.

Auxilio's wings beat heavily in the air as he dodged another swipe of his enemy's sword. He parried with a blow of his own, striking the hard plate armor of the Demon opposing him.

Shadows flew overhead, momentarily distracting him and allowing his adversary to strike at an unprotected part of his body. The blade bit deeply into his arm, separating skin and flesh. His scream of agony pierced the skies. His wings fluttered as he tried to regain control over his body which was wracked with painful spasms. He lost altitude, the ground hurtled toward him as he desperately tried to regain control of his wings.

The mocking laughter of the Demon who had felled him chased his ears on the wind. Auxilio closed his eyes, waiting for the inevitable. Was this the end? Angels and Demons were immortal, but serious injuries could cease their immortal lives in a single beat.

Auxilio realized his time may well have come. His thoughts drifted to Ebony, how they'd had so little time together. He prepared himself for the final strike against the ground which would end him, but instead found himself landing on something much softer than concrete. Strong arms wound their way around his torso, wings flapped powerfully around him.

Auxilio opened his eyes to see Thomas's face, strained with his additional weight.The Angel's dark-tinged wings flapped against the bright sunlight in an effort to keep them both airborne. "I'm not dead." Auxilio's voice was laced with pain.

"Not yet. Ebony would kill me if I let anything happen to you." Thomas grinned. Behind him a Demon descended, his sword out and held in an easy grip.

"Behind you." Auxilio warned Thomas of the approaching enemy.

"Thomas, are you all right? Does he live?" The Demon shouted to them.

"Yes, we're fine Decimus!" Thomas shouted back as they headed toward the ground at a more sedate pace than Auxilio's previously deadly hurtle. Thomas placed the injured Demon on the ground.

Above them Decimus' forces joined the fray. War cries and falling feathers continued. Thomas tore a strip from his shirt and bound Auxilio's bleeding arm, making sure he would survive.

"You and your friends arrived just in time. We were rapidly losing and now it appears we will be victorious in this battle." Auxilio watched the battle on high.

"Yes, Decimus has a few battles beneath his belt. He was one of Marius' soldiers. His best, if Marius was to be believed before Decimus killed him. He tried to convince Decimus to return to his side and serve him; Decimus wouldn't have any of it."

"So he was killed by his own soldier." Auxilio continued watching the skies as the battle broke. The last two enemy warriors fled, chased by four Demons and an Angel from Thomas and Decimus' group. "How ironic…" he muttered, realizing their situation was similar. He too would be killing his former leader.

Decimus flew down to Auxilio and Thomas' side. Bloodied and sweat-streaked, he smiled. "That was some fun, when can we do it again?" He flopped down beside Thomas.

"Soon. Very soon." Auxilio answered.

15.

The women worked hard to help the Demons and Angels clean up, while the human men kept watch for any more incursions against them.

Auxilio sighed as Ebony fretted and tended to his wounds. He accepted her fussing over him in good humor. "Woman, I'm fine."

She slapped him on the bandaged wound, causing him to grunt and wince at the stinging pain which lingered. "You are a damned fool, almost getting yourself killed like that. What would I do without you, Auxilio?" The dam burst, Ebony fell against his bare chest and sobbed. His strong hands surrounded her, soothing her, stroking her back as she wept.

"Ebony, my love. I am alright, but I owe Thomas my life. He saved me when I fell." He looked lovingly at the woman in his arms, "We have much to plan for. I think it would be a good idea if we discussed and settled the plan now we have Decimus and his friends with us." He pulled away slightly, and noted her tear-streaked and reddened face. He lifted her chin with a forefinger and caressed her bottom lip with his thumb. "Go get cleaned up and we will all meet on the concourse to get this plan underway."

She nodded, and turned away.

Grace watched from within the circle of Thomas' arms. She too had given him a piece of her mind when he had returned, but she had thanked him when she'd learned the news of his timely arrival and saving of Auxilio.

The two Demons, and Thomas, converged on the concourse of the station where the others in their groups joined them. There were only three or four sets of white wings amongst the black.

A chair was placed so Auxilio could sit. A gash on his leg had been overlooked due to the pain he'd felt in his arm and the adrenaline rush during the battle. It had been tended to, but it remained painful and troublesome to stand on. Thomas and Decimus stood on either side as Auxilio explained the plan to take down Maximus to the gathered Demons and Angels.

"Three days hence, we shall begin to head out in small groups. The last group will consist of Decimus, Thomas, Karius, and Marcellus, who will be *escorting* myself, Ebony and Grace to the gates of the city as prisoners. Decimus will claim to be a hunter who has taken us all as his captives after hearing of the bounty on my head. We will be bound in chains." He looked pointedly at Ebony, who began to shake her head.

"No, I won't be bound again." Her voice was high and tight.

Auxilio stood and hobbled to her, taking her in his arms. "If there were any other way, my love, you know I would take it. We can leave the chains off until absolutely necessary, but we need them to keep the ruse." He stroked her hair softly.

Grace watched, a concerned expression on her face. Auxilio held her sister tightly, securely. She understood he wanted to keep her safe, but this plan was going to break her sister a little more than she already was.

Ebony projected a tough, no-nonsense exterior, but on the inside, Grace had the feeling her sister was shattered emotionally by her ordeal at the hands of Maximus. She swallowed the bitter taste in her mouth. "What do we need to do to get ready?" Grace asked him.

Auxilio smiled. Thomas placed a hand on her shoulder and squeezed reassuringly as the Demon explained further. "You will need to prepare yourself mentally. Maximus enjoys exhibitionism, gore, and some forms of torture with his sex. He is quite depraved in his tastes. There's only so much I can tell you to prepare yourself for this meeting, and we *will* be meeting him. I'll have a weapon concealed on my person, it's a blessed dagger that will kill him as long as he takes it in the heart."

"The same as the one we used to kill Marius," Thomas said.

"The very same blade." Decimus reached into a satchel at his side, removed a velvet cover, the dagger's handle sticking out. He pulled the leather sheath from the satchel and removed the velvet cover. The silver blade shone under the lights of the concourse. "This is what will kill him. You'll need to get up close and personal with him."

"Let's do this." Ebony's face darkened with a hatred Grace hadn't known her little sister possessed.

Auxilio kissed her head. "So eager, my little one."

The group of humans, Demons and Angels waited at the grand doors to Maximus' fortress, the City's former town hall. The classic Romanesque style of the building was beautiful but also foreboding. Grisly displays of defaced human bodies adorned the columns, tied to the concrete and faux-marble structures with barbed wire.

Grace glanced at the damaged faces. Features frozen in bloody rictuses, there was no serenity in the deaths of these people. The six Demon guards watched their little group of eight as they approached. Thomas and Decimus led them, playing the part of bounty hunters. Auxilio was bound right behind them, his chains had a weak link he could easily break.

Grace and Ebony were both chained hand and foot. Grace's collar was again around her neck, while Ebony had a new one, pilfered from a pet store. A length of chain went from one collar to the other, then to Thomas' hand.

Two of the Demon guards opened the grand doors and led them inside. The darkness of the building enveloped them as they entered. They had not been stopped anywhere except at the gate to the inner city where they explained to the humans, they had a bounty to collect from Maximus.

Their footsteps echoed through the dark hallway, the soft glow of candles at their feet didn't reach the ceiling of the hallway. It gave Grace a feeling of deep, dark despair as they walked towards the grand hall. The eyes of guards posted through the hallway greeted them with airs of indifference or lustful hunger for the sisters.

Their guides stopped at another set of doors. They pulled them open, revealing the large grand hall. The group was ushered inside. Along the walls of the grand hall, women were chained naked. Soft and compliant eyes watched their passage as the slave girls sat on cushions and mattresses.

Ebony's body trembled beside Grace as their feet moved across the tiled floor. Before them sat a large chair, it looked like it belonged in a church or even a king's throne room. It was covered in a large, furry throw rug. Metal brackets were bolted to the legs and two attached chains coiled on the floor.

Grace's eyes settled on the figure seated on the throne. Her heart pounded as she felt the fear creeping into her body. One of the largest Demons she had ever laid eyes on, sat comfortably at his ease. A being of great power and prowess sat before them, his lips curled in a victorious smirk. He rose, powerful muscles bunching and shifting as he moved with cat-like grace to their group. He pushed through Decimus and Thomas, shoved aside Auxilio and stood before Grace and Ebony.

"Welcome home." His fingers traced Ebony's jawline. He turned his eyes to Grace. "Ah, Grace, such a beautiful name for one such as you. Fitting, very fitting." He took the girls' chained hands and led them back through the group.

"What about our price?" Decimus asked as Thomas shifted forward to try to stop Maximus from taking the girls. Decimus' hand on his arm barely stopped the Angel.

"Your price?" Maximus turned to regard them. "Your price is your heads, adorning the entry. I know your Angel is the one who killed Tobias." He smirked, as he handed the chained girls over to another Demon who locked them in the chains attached to the throne. Grace looked up in fear as Maximus towered over them. He smiled down at her, his hand caressing her cheek.

"I am grateful you brought both girls to me, especially my Ebony. She is quite special as I'm sure you know, Auxilio." He caressed Ebony's cheek.

Auxilio roared, unable to take Maximus' pawing of his woman any longer. His body trembled in anger as he snapped the chains at their weak link. Thomas, Decimus and their three companions broke apart, each pulling a sword from their sheaths, Auxilio was unarmed. He stormed toward Maximus as the guards in the hall raced to attack.

Grace scrambled over to Ebony who was terrified. "It's okay." She tried to soothe her sister with a hug. "We're going to be fine."

"And what about our men?" Ebony whispered, fear choked her voice.

Grace watched as the battle commenced.

Auxilio threw himself against Maximus, blind fury fuelling his flight toward his former lord and friend. His hard body smashed against that of the larger Demon, the force knocking them both to the ground.

Maximus grunted beneath him, his hands capturing Auxilio's as they went for Maximus' neck. "You were a fool; you should have stayed with me. You could have been a great leader. I even had a small town for you to take over, but no, you wanted to take what was mine." He snarled, pulled his knees up under Auxilio and pushed, throwing the Demon off him.

Auxilio sailed through the air and slammed against a wall near a frightened slave girl. Maximus charged toward him and reached out. He grabbed Maximus's shirt and using his momentum, changed his direction out into the fray, following the flight of his enemy's body.

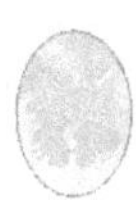

Thomas battled a Demon, his sword clashed against the metal of his opponent's blade. The room had grown hot and stifling with the grunts and cries of battle, the scent of sweat, blood and other bodily fluids that were spilled from eviscerated stomachs. The air was thick with the combined stench. Fear and anger permeated every pore of his body as he battled, slew and sought another to kill or maim.

He worked his way closer to Decimus who was dispatching another Demon. The butchered wing he had sliced from the screaming Demon slid to the floor in a bloody mess of black feathers and torn flesh. Decimus quickly beheaded him and turned to Thomas. Their compatriots were fighting other guards as Thomas and Decimus fought their way closer to where Auxilio and Maximus were locked in combat.

The Angel and his Demon friend were attacked by another pair of guards and distracted from Auxilio's battle.

A heart-wrenching scream halted the battle.

Auxilio was raised above Maximus, a sword thrust through his body. Maximus held him aloft, his body hard and flush against the hilt of the bloody sword. Maximus grinned wickedly as he lowered Auxilio's body and let him slide off the blade onto the floor.

Thomas's roar broke the stillness. Ebony's sobbing and screams reverberated through the hall as both Thomas and Decimus raced toward the sneering form of Maximus. Thomas pulled the Blessed Dagger from its sheath.

It glinted in the dim light of the hall, silver in the candlelight, hungry for the taste of Demon flesh.

Maximus' mocking laughter fuelled his fire. "Do you really believe you can harm me with that?"

"I will redeem you unto death," Thomas snarled.

Decimus plowed into Maximus, throwing him off-balance and to the ground. Thomas followed, the deadly blade firmly clasped in his hand as he lowered the blade with deadly precision into the enemy's chest.

Maximus' eyes widened as the pain of the Blessed Dagger burned through him, his breath heaved once, twice and he shuddered as his heart stopped.

Thomas wrenched the dagger free of the still form of Maximus. Around them the dead Demon's guards stood.

"Auxilio!" Ebony's cry shocked them from their thoughts. She stood, the length of chain binding her to Maximus' throne tight behind her. Grace stood a few steps behind at the taut length of her own chain.

"Free them." Thomas nodded to Decimus before moving quickly to Auxilio's side. The blood pooled beneath him, there was only one thing he could do, and little time left to do it. He wondered at his choice, would it be for gain or loss?

What would it mean for him, to make such a heavy sacrifice? He sighed heavily. His decision made, he plucked the last pure white feather from his wings and placed it over the bloody wound on Auxilio's still chest.

Then he did something he had not done in a very long time.

He prayed.

To be continued in The Demon's Bargain.

(Auxilio and Ebony's story)

Thank you for reading Angel's Redemption, Book Two in the Redemption of the Fallen Series!

If you'd like to connect with me, you can find me on Facebook.

https://www.facebook.com/scarlettjrose/